"Anna, let's go to the boat."

"Why?" Lucas had avoided the boathouse like the plague until now.

"I'll explain in a minute."

Anna did as requested and followed Lucas down the path that led to the boathouse. As they neared the building, Lucas's steps faltered for a brief moment before he squared his shoulders, as though approaching the boathouse equaled going into battle. "Lucas, could I ask you a question?"

"Sure," he said, but never looked at her, just kept his eyes on the door to the building.

"What's the deal with you and your father? Why is it so tense and formal between you?"

"Because I killed my brother."

Books by Lynette Eason

Love Inspired Suspense

Lethal Deception
River of Secrets
Holiday Illusion

LYNETTE EASON

Lynette Eason grew up in Greenville, South Carolina. Her home church, Northgate Baptist, had a tremendous influence on her during her early years. She credits Christian parents and dedicated Sunday school teachers for her acceptance of Christ at the tender age of eight. Even as a young girl, she knew she wanted her life to reflect the love of Jesus.

Lynette attended the University of South Carolina in Columbia, then moved to Spartanburg to attend Converse College where she obtained her master's degree in education. During this time, she met the boy next door, Jack Eason—and married him. Jack is the executive director of the Sound of Light Ministries. Lynette and Jack have two precious children, Lauryn, eight years old, and Will, who is six. She and Jack are members of New Life Baptist Fellowship Church in Boiling Springs, South Carolina, where Jack serves as the worship leader and Lynette teaches Sunday school to the four- and five-year olds.

Holiday
ILLUSION

Lynette Eason

Steeple
Hill®

Published by Steeple Hill Books™

CM

STEEPLE HILL BOOKS

Steeple
Hill®

ISBN-13: 978-0-373-44316-1
ISBN-10:   0-373-44316-1

HOLIDAY ILLUSION

www.SteepleHill.com

Printed in U.S.A.

His divine power has given us everything we need for life and godliness, through our knowledge of him who called us by his own glory and goodness. Through these he has given us his very great and precious promises, so that through them you may participate in the divine nature and escape the corruption in the world caused by evil desires.

—*2 Peter* 1:3–4

To Jesus Christ, who lets me do this.
I love You, Lord.

My grandmother, Freda Trowbridge,
died February 2, 2008. I'm so grateful she got
to read my first published book, *Lethal Deception.*
She won't get to finish the series this side of heaven,
so I decided I wanted to make a special dedication
to the memory of my grandparents:

Paternal grandparents: Lewis Carroll, Sr.
and Kate Bexley Barker

Maternal grandparents: Cary Eugene and
Freda Jackson Trowbridge

Thanks for being godly men and women. I know
Jesus found it easy to say to each one of you,
"Well done, my good and faithful servants."

And, of course, thanks always to my family
and friends who make it possible for me to write.
I couldn't do it without you.

One more special thanks goes to Barbara Lollis, one
of my childhood Sunday school teachers. I've lost
count of how many books you've bought to give
away. I know my sales numbers are going to look
great thanks to your efforts. God bless you!

ONE

The boy was going to die.

Lucas stared down at Paulo, the nine-year-old child in the hospital bed, listening to the heart monitor blip and beep, the sound echoing through his brain as though amplified by a hundred microphones. An innocent child with no one in the world to care whether he lived or died—except the staff at the Amazon Orphanage in Tefe, Brazil.

With compassion crimping his heart, Lucas reached out a hand to brush a finger down the silky soft skin that, in the absence of a miracle, would never know a whisker. His knuckle bumped the oxygen tube attached to Paulo's nose and he stirred, eyelids flickering up, down, then back up. The brown eyes focused in on Lucas, and the boy smiled.

"Hey, Paulo. How are you doing? Hanging in there?" The Portuguese fell from Lucas's tongue with practiced ease.

"Sim," the boy breathed. "I will get a new heart soon, right, Doctor?"

"Soon, Paulo, soon." I hope. But here in Brazil, it wasn't likely. Even in some of the bigger cities where health care was improving, a heart transplant was a rare occurrence. The boy's best hope lay in the United States. He'd had Paulo on the list there for four months now. Paulo's time was running out.

"If I don't, I will die, yes?" Speaking drained his energy, but the look in Paulo's eyes told Lucas he'd better be honest. Paulo knew all about death as he came from the slums of Brazil. A place that made the slums of America look like high-class living.

Instead of answering with a yes, Lucas asked, "How would you like to take a trip to America?"

Brown eyes shot wide, hope mingling with disbelief as he stared up his beloved doctor. "America?"

Lucas nodded. "That's the only way you're going to be able to get a new heart."

"When?"

"As soon as I can arrange for someone to take you."

"Will I get to build a snowman? I've always wanted to build a snowman. And see snow on Christmas day."

It was all Lucas could do to keep the tears from his eyes. He'd been a doctor for a few years, even had patients he'd become fond of, but Paulo… He stroked the boy's hair. "Sure thing, Paulo, as soon as we get to America and get your new heart, we'll build a snowman for Christmas. It'll be here before we know it."

"He needs to go to the States?"

Lucas whirled to face the quiet voice from the door. "Anna." As always, his heart kicked into overtime as he watched her come into the room. She'd been his best friend for three years, but lately he found himself wondering if their friendship could become something more. And yet, he was hesitant to push it further for a couple of reasons. One, he knew her faith in God was her mainstay, and he didn't put stock in religion. You could depend on yourself and that was it. Still, he had to admit, as he'd watched her over the past few years, he was becoming more and more interested in God, simply because he saw something in her he'd never seen in anyone else. And two, she was hiding something, holding something back. And until he figured out what that was…

Short, sassy curls framed a perfect oval-shaped face that held stunning blue eyes, high cheekbones and full lips. He watched those lips stretch into a sad smile as she zeroed in on the sick child. "Hi there, Paulo."

She didn't ask how the boy was feeling—it was pretty obvious. Walking around to the other side of the bed, she leaned down to press a kiss to his brown cheek, brushing black curls back from his forehead with her right hand.

The sound of Paulo's rasping breaths filled the room, but his entire countenance lit up when he saw her. "Miss Anna, you came to see me. Thank you. I love you. I'm going to build a snowman for Christmas, will you help me?"

Her eyes went wide as her breath caught on a suppressed sob. "Oh, Paulo, honey, I love you, too. And if we're together on Christmas Day, playing in the snow, you bet I'll help. Just try and stop me."

Lucas reached across Paulo to take Anna's hand and squeeze. Slender fingers gripped his, her throat working, lips trembling. Lucas watched her gain control and stroke Paulo's cheek, much in the same way he'd done earlier.

Paulo's lashes fluttered shut, sleep claiming him after the effort he'd just expended. Anna's blue gaze fixed itself on Lucas. "When?"

"As soon as possible. A week max. He's fading pretty fast. I've had him on the list for a while and he's moved up to the number two spot. I think it's time to go." He stood and motioned for Anna to follow him into the hall. "I made some phone calls and managed to get a plane on its way. A craft specifically designed for transporting medically fragile patients. It's got all the bells and whistles, almost better than an operating room. I just need someone to take him."

"Where's he going? Why didn't you tell me?"

Lucas blew out a sigh, rubbing a hand through his reddish-blond hair. "I'm sorry. I haven't really had a chance. All this came together so fast."

"No, it's okay," she rushed to assure him. "I want what's best for Paulo. I knew he was on the list, I'm just a little surprised it's actually happening, that's all. Where are you taking him?"

"Rocking Wave Beach, South Carolina. They've offered to do the surgery for free. If you can travel with Paulo, then I feel confident about sending him to one of the best hospitals in the country—Travis Memorial." He studied her, wondering if he should ask. But the thought of leaving her for an extended period of time did weird things to his emotions. He took a chance and blurted, "I know that since the orphanage is considered Paulo's guardian, one of the higher-level staff will have to accompany him, and I was hoping that would be you. If I can arrange it, would you be willing to go with me?"

"Rocking Wave Beach?" She didn't like the squeak in her voice but couldn't seem to help it. "I'd rather go anywhere than there. What about another hospital, in another state?"

Lucas frowned, hope drooping at her negative

response. "No, my buddy from college has offered to do this at no expense. Everything is already arranged."

"And you want me to go with you?"

"Yes. Rocking Wave is perfect. It has one of the best heart-transplant hospitals in America. I pulled some strings and got Paulo lined up on a transplant list and he's almost at the top. There's only one other person on the list who's as sick as Paulo. And the surgery will be free."

She narrowed her gaze, rubbed her chin. Nightmares from her past paraded through her thoughts, mocking her, daring her. Could she finally face her fear?

Lord, what do I do? Taking a deep breath, she said, "Okay, I'll go with him…you." Almost as though to reinforce the thought, she gave a decisive nod. "Yes, I'll go."

Lucas scrubbed a hand down a cheek. "You will? You're sure? He'll need round-the-clock care until he arrives at the hospital."

"That's where you come in, right?"

Lucas furrowed his brow. The indecisiveness on his face made her wonder what was going through his mind. "Yes. I grew up not too far from Rocking Wave Beach."

She blinked at the sudden switch in topic. What did his hometown have to do with Paulo? "So you said. I remember you telling me that during one of our little talks. Haven, North Carolina, right?"

"Yep."

Home to the comfortably wealthy about two hours from where she'd grown up. A complete and utter contrast to her childhood of poverty and struggle. Could she really go back there? To the place where her life had fallen apart?

She had no doubt that Shawn de Chastelain, the man who wanted her dead, didn't have a clue where she was right now or she'd have seen evidence of him a long time ago. But while he may be in jail, he still had his connections to the outside world. If she returned and he found out, her life would be in danger. She'd just have to keep him from finding out. She could go, be with Paulo, and when he sufficiently recovered, return home with him. Piece of cake, right?

Maybe.

Anna said her goodbyes to Paulo and told Lucas, "Let me know when you have the official dates. I'll start making arrangements to leave."

She left the hospital to head back to the orphanage, her mind swirling with memories breaking to the forefront of her thoughts. Pulling into her parking spot, she leaned her head against the steering wheel to gather herself together before climbing out of the Jeep.

Shawn de Chastelain and Rocking Wave Beach. The combination was enough to send her heart crashing against her chest in sheer terror. Bringing images from the dungeons of her mind to swirl in front of her, causing bile to rise to the back of her throat. She swallowed hard and gave up fighting the memories.

Four years ago, she'd been undercover on a sting operation for the FBI, and she'd barely escaped the city with her life. Just being in the same state would be diving headlong into the memories that became nightmares the moment she lay her head on the pillow at night.

Anna sucked in a deep breath. *Lord, I can't go back.*

I'm not strong enough to face those memories. Just setting foot back in the United States will bring it all back and I don't want to remember!

Chewing her lip, she pondered the fact that Rocking Wave Beach was a pretty big city. Surely, with a population of a couple hundred thousand, she wouldn't run into the killer that stalked her dreams; the one she'd allowed to nose-dive her career and almost cause her to have a nervous breakdown. For a long time, she'd hidden, bogged down by depression, despair dogging her every waking moment. It had taken a long time for her to stop wishing the bullet that had pierced her uterus and left her barren had been about a foot higher to go right through her heart.

But God had allowed her to live. By trusting Him to be faithful, to get her through that awful time, she'd beaten the depression and He'd led her to the children at the orphanage in Brazil. Children who had no mother, no father and no one to tell them they were beautiful and loved. But she'd done that and slowly she'd healed…at least she thought she had.

Until she'd been asked to return to the city that haunted her dreams.

The thought brought into clarity the image of the man she'd helped put away.

Shawn de Chastelain with the military crew cut, strong jaw, bright white teeth outlined by firm, full lips that stretched into the smile that often graced the lifestyle section of the Rocking Wave Beach newspaper. His muscular shoulders had looked like they could support the world's burdens. He also had a heart of evil, the soul of a killer.

Only he'd never been convicted of the murder she'd

witnessed. The FBI had gotten him on tax evasion but not murder. Yet. She shuddered, pressed a hand to her abdomen and prayed for the strength to do this. Prayed for the courage to face her fear and defeat it.

Turning off her thoughts, she finally left the car and entered the front door to the orphanage. Instead of stopping by her office, she went straight for her small suite of rooms located just down the hall. Stepping inside, she paused and looked around. Nothing out of place, everything organized just so. She grabbed a can of soda from the minifridge.

Booting up her computer, she was relieved to see the Internet connection giving off a strong signal. With all the storms out here, the connection was intermittent at best. A few clicks brought up her homepage which was the *Rocking Wave Beach News*. She straightened. More news about de Chastelain. He was being released… soon. No exact date yet.

Anna took another sip and gripped the can so hard she crunched it. The crackling noise and cold liquid running down her fingers jerked her from her memories. Breathing hard, she set the can down, wiping her hand on her jeans, ignoring the stickiness.

What had happened to that evidence she'd found? She'd lost track of how many times she'd silently asked herself that question. Her colleague Justin didn't have an answer, either. The FBI agents who'd come in behind her should have found that memory card with no trouble. The sting operation had gone off like clockwork…at least up to the point where she'd been shot and they'd realized someone had slipped through the cracks. So, who had messed up? Justin didn't know, and she was going to drive herself insane running it over and over in her mind.

Gritting her teeth, she shut down the computer. It didn't matter. She'd done her job, paid the price for doing it. She was in a different line of work now, didn't have to worry about men who killed, didn't have to wonder when she stepped outside whether a bullet would pierce her flesh. She definitely didn't miss the stress and tension of the job…or the adrenaline high, the satisfaction of a job well done, the knowledge she'd made a difference in keeping someone safe for one more day. She didn't miss it at all.

Much. Terribly much. Well, maybe a little. If she could get over her fear…

She was going back for Paulo. Just Paulo. Because she would need to be there to sign papers and offer him love and support. And that was it. Period.

"How's he doing?" Anna asked as she settled onto the love seat beside Lucas, two glasses of lemonade fresh from the fridge clutched in each hand. She ignored the pitter-patter her heart made whenever she was close to him or thought about him or pictured them together at some point in the future or… Someday, maybe… *Uh-uh. Don't go there, Anna.*

Ella, one of the orphanage staff who'd volunteered to go along as an extra pair of hands, snoozed on the pullout sofa off to the side. The plane cruised smoothly through the clouds at thirty-five thousand feet, due to land at Rocking Wave Beach Airport in approximately one hour. They'd flown all night, the two pilots taking turns sleeping and flying. She'd just had a nap in the queen-size bed at the back of the plane and felt refreshed in spite of what lay ahead.

Lucas looked up and took the glass of lemonade. "Thanks. He's sleeping right now."

"He's such a special kid. He's been a real trouper. I just hope…" She bit her lip, looking down at the plush carpet.

"Yeah, me, too." Lucas set the glass on the end table, rising to check Paulo's vitals one more time. "An ambulance will be waiting at the airport for us. I'll get him loaded on then get a rental car while you and Ella ride with him to the hospital. I'll meet you all there."

"Don't you want to ride with him? I don't mind getting the car."

"No, I have something I need to take care of. He'll be in good care. My friend Mark Priestly is the heart surgeon on this case. He's going to be in the ambulance waiting on us."

Anna looked curious about what he needed to take care of, but didn't ask, just nodded.

Slightly less than an hour later, they were on the ground, and rolling Paulo into the ambulance. Lucas greeted Mark warmly. "Hey buddy, how are you? I can't tell you how much I appreciate you doing this."

The tall, slenderly built doctor had a head of shaggy blond curls and smiling hazel eyes. He looked more like a surfer than the top-notch, highly in demand surgeon that he was. He grabbed Lucas in a bear hug. "Man, it's been forever." Concern touched his eyes. "You back for good?"

Lucas shrugged, ignoring the meaning behind the question. "We'll see."

"Yeah, and we'll talk, too."

Lucas motioned to Anna. "This is the lady I was telling you about. Anna Freeman, this is Mark Priestly."

Mark turned his smile to Anna, holding out a hand

graced with slender yet strong fingers. "Nice to meet you. You're as beautiful as Lucas said."

Anna blushed, which Lucas found extremely charming. He shot his buddy a glance that said *watch it,* then introduced Ella, who smiled shyly and shook the doctor's hand.

Anna, Mark and Ella climbed into the ambulance and Mark turned professional in the blink of an eye, checking Paulo's vitals, reading through his chart and asking a dozen questions. Once he was satisfied he waved Lucas on. "We'll see you there." Lucas watched the ambulance pull away.

Sighing, he shivered, tugging his leather jacket tighter around himself. Gripping his cell phone, he wondered if he should even bother checking in with his family. After all, it had been close to three years since he'd even spoken to his father. Three years since his father had blamed him for his brother's death. Lucas shook off the thoughts, clipped his phone back into its case and headed for the rental car counter. Four days ago, when he'd called to let his family know he'd be coming home, Ted, the family chauffeur had been thrilled to hear from him and had offered to send a car around to the airport. Lucas had refused because, until he had more time to get a feel for how things were going to go at home and with his father, he didn't want to be without immediate transportation. A rental car would be just fine.

"Excuse me, sir."

Lucas looked up to see a fresh-faced teen dressed in the popular tradition of faded frayed blue jeans, and a cropped top revealing a pierced navel. Didn't the girl know it was the last week in October and unseasonably cold?

Hiding his thoughts, he asked, "Yes?"

"We're on a mission trip and I just wanted to give you this. You look like you could use a friend." She handed over the little slip of paper.

A tract. Great, just what he needed. He forced a smile. "Thanks. Good luck with your trip."

A beautiful smile crossed her lips to mesh with the peace written in her eyes. Eyes that reminded him of Anna even though this girl's eyes were chocolate-brown and Anna's were sky-blue.

"I don't need luck," she said. "I've got God."

Well, since I don't have God, I guess I'll have to stick with luck.

Why that thought depressed him, he wasn't sure, but instead of dwelling on it, he crossed to the car rental place to get in line. A dancing reindeer with a red nose greeted him as he approached the counter bobbing in time to "Jingle Bell Rock." He shook his head. Not even Thanksgiving yet, and Christmas waved to him from every direction.

The trash can to his right caught his attention while the tract burned a hole in the palm of his hand. Curling his fingers around the paper, he started to slam-dunk it when, from the corner of his eye, he caught sight of a blue-jean-clad leg jiggling in time to the music in the girl's head. She was still watching him. Instead of scoring a two-pointer, he slid the paper into the front pocket of his jacket. He'd toss it later when she wasn't around. No use in hurting her feelings even if she was deluded into thinking God cared about anything she did.

Finally, keys in hand, he headed for his car, tugging his phone from the clip on his side as he walked, his other hand pulling his rolling suitcase along behind him. Anna's and Ella's things would be shipped to the hospital within the hour.

Frigid air greeted him as he stepped outside, nearly sucking every last drop of oxygen from his shocked lungs. He'd forgotten how cold it could get even in the South. Used to eighty-plus-degree weather year-round, the fifty-two degrees he was now shivering in seemed to make his blood freeze mid-flow.

Fingers trembling, he pressed the remote unlock for his compact little car and climbed in. The heater finally going full blast, he pulled out of the parking garage and stopped at the stop sign. Tapping his fingers on the wheel, he finally decided it was now or never to ask the question he'd been wondering for the past three years.

Pulling out his phone, he dialed his father's number.

"Hello?" The voice sounded weaker, not quite containing the strength it had had three years ago.

"Hello, Father, it's me, Lucas."

Silence.

"Father?"

A throat clearing was his only clue that the line hadn't been disconnected.

"Lucas. Well, I must say, son, you've taken me quite by surprise." The voice was stronger now, although Lucas heard the shock in the words. "May I ask the purpose of your call?" The British accent had never faded from his father's voice in all the time he'd been in the United States. The formal stiffness the man injected into his tone was enough to intimidate the most stalwart. Fortunately, Lucas was immune.

"Yes sir, I've had a question that's been bothering

me for the last three years or so, and I've finally decided to ask it."

"Very well. What is it?" Typical. Straight to the point. No, how are you? Where've you been? What have you been doing with your life since you've been gone? Old hurt and new anger shot through him.

"Did you really mean it when you said it should have been me that died in the fire instead of Lance?"

TWO

Anna sat by the bedside of the sick boy, praying like she'd never prayed before. For Paulo, for herself, for Lucas. And for the strength to face her fear. She would *not* think about the past right now. Ella would be back in a few minutes. She'd taken a short break to run a few personal errands before ensconcing herself by Paulo's side.

Reaching for the backpack Anna carried in lieu of a purse, she grabbed her Bible and turned to the verse that had become her mantra over the last four years. *God has not given us the spirit of fear, but of power, and of love, and of a sound mind.* She whispered the verse to herself, praying, *God, I know the time has come to face the past, but I've got to be honest with You. I'm scared. Really, really scared…and I don't want to be. Don't let the fear handicap me. Could You please keep Your hand of protection on whatever it is I'm getting myself back into?*

"Hey."

She looked up to see Lucas standing in the door looking rumpled and wonderful, his reddish-blond hair windblown…or maybe it was messy from the number of times he'd shoved his fingers through it. No matter. He still looked good, safe, a comfort zone. She wondered what he'd do if she ran to him and threw her arms around him. Better not find out. Instead, she cleared her throat and asked, "Hey, yourself. Did you get your errand run?"

When his jaw started twitching, she figured that was the wrong question to ask.

"Something like that," he muttered. "More like an overdue phone call."

"Ah." She refused to press. He'd tell her eventually; he always did. At least he used to. "What did Mark say?"

"He agrees we need to change two of Paulo's meds. There are newer, more effective ones on the market now. I didn't even know about them until two weeks ago." He shook his head. "I've been out of touch too long."

"Lucas, you can't blame yourself. Paulo arrived on our doorstep as sick as any child I've ever seen. But he seemed perfectly healthy after recovering from that virus. There's no way any of us could have known it affected his heart."

"Mentally, I know that. I did the best I could. But still…" He trailed off, shaking his head. "I can't help wondering if I missed something, should have suggested bringing him to the U.S. sooner."

"Brazil is so far behind in health care. If you hadn't acted as you did, Paulo would be gone by now. Unfortunately, he's a product of his country…and very, very blessed that you were there when he needed you."

Lucas slipped an arm around her shoulders for a squeeze then let her go. "Thanks. You always know the right thing to say."

Anna blinked. Not that she and Lucas hadn't shared a friendly hug or two, but it always surprised her. He wasn't normally the most demonstrative person. Growing up in a strict British household, he'd told her affectionate moments were few and far between.

"Sure," she gulped. "You're welcome."

Lucas leaned over Paulo one more time while Anna stepped to the side, eyeing the phone on the nightstand by the bed. She took a deep breath, wondering if she should call Justin and just…check in. Let him know she was back in the States; get an update on de Chastelain. The old adage keep your friends close, keep your enemies closer ran through her mind.

"What's going on in that head of yours, Anna?"

Lucas's insightful question startled her. Chewing her lip, she debated how much she could tell him. She could just shrug the question off, but found herself wanting him to know. Wanting to confide in him. Open up to him. Carrying her burden alone had become so tiresome. "I was just thinking about how I ended up in Brazil. I told you a little about it."

"You just said you had to get away from home for a while. That you'd witnessed a crime and didn't feel safe."

"Right, well, it's a little more in-depth than that."

"Okay." He held out his hand. "Why don't we walk down to the cafeteria and get a bite to eat. You can explain over our savory hospital food."

Anna was about to agree when the door opened. Dr. Mark Priestly entered, followed by an orderly pushing a gurney. "I thought Paulo might like a roommate. Sometimes it can get awfully lonely when you can't get out of bed. The television will probably get old fast."

A boy about Paulo's age lay on the gurney. Wide green eyes took in his new surroundings. A shock of red hair stood on end and the freckles on his pasty white cheeks appeared three-dimensional. The portable heart monitor rode in front of him, the oxygen tube blended into his face. A worried mother, the last to enter the room, was in her early thirties and the feminine version of her son.

Mark spoke up. "Missy, I'd like to introduce you to some friends of mine. This is Anna Freeman and Lucas Bennett. They're here with Paulo who's over there sleeping." He gestured toward the newcomers. "This is Missy and Andy Spears. Andy's waiting on a new heart, too. He's ten."

Anna shook the woman's hand. "I wish it were under other circumstances, but it's nice to meet you."

Giving a wan smile, Missy shrugged. "I'm just glad Andy will have someone to talk to…when he feels like talking. He seems to be getting weaker all the time." Tears appeared but didn't fall. Just as quickly, they were gone. Anna suspected Missy probably went through this many times during her days—and nights.

"I know Paulo will appreciate it. I'm sure the two of them will hit it right off, although Paulo is very weak, too. I don't know how much talking he'll do."

"It doesn't matter." Missy stroked her son's red hair. "As long as he's willing to listen, my Andy will keep the conversation going."

"Okay guys," Mark said from the door. "I'm off to check on other patients, but let me know if there's anything else you need. I'll be back this afternoon."

"Thanks, Dr. Priestly," Missy all but whispered, and sat on the bed beside her son who was fumbling with the remote.

Lucas waved to Missy and stepped outside to speak privately with Mark. Anna turned to Missy. "We were just going down to grab a bite to eat. Would you like to join us?" Although she really needed to talk to Lucas alone, she felt sorry for the sad-eyed mom.

"No, we're fine. I'll stay here with Andy. Thanks, though."

"Anytime. I'm sure I'll see you later."

Stepping from the room, she was just in time to watch Mark disappear around the corner at the end of the hall. Turning to Lucas, she said, "Ready now?"

"Ready."

Anna took a bite of her chicken salad sandwich eyeing Lucas while she chewed. How much should she tell him? What would he think about her when he found out? She dropped her focus to her plate.

Lucas set his cheeseburger aside and raised a red-tinged golden brow. "So?"

"All right, here goes. I'm an *ex*-FBI agent. I quit four years ago, signed my resignation and never looked back." *At least not any more than I could help.*

Shock seemed to hold Lucas captive. She went on before he could ask the questions she saw gathering on his lips. "A little over four years ago, I was working undercover as an au pair for a wealthy, big-name family here in Rocking Wave Beach. It was supposed to be a routine sting operation. I was there to get information about this guy who was involved in all kinds of bad stuff. It was a well-known fact that he worked from home, and our main target was his office computer. Anyway, I waited until my 'employer' left for a business meeting in India. I got on his computer and went to work." Talking about Chastelain was hard for her.

"I think you left a few details out of the many talks we had in Brazil." He cleared his throat. "So what did you find?"

"Nothing."

"Huh?"

"Nothing terribly incriminating. Not for the big stuff we were after. There were a lot of e-mails containing numbers. Written almost in something like code."

"What did that mean?"

"I wasn't sure, but I had a gut feeling it had to do with money. I needed one of our analysts to go over them, so I forwarded them to her, then erased my 'footprints.' I just had to take the chance he wouldn't realize someone had been on his computer. Later, we figured out the numbers were the ones entered into a set of books. Doctored books."

"And that's how you guys were able to arrest him? For illegal books?"

"Yes, but I wanted more. I *knew* there was more. He was reportedly into all kinds of things. Thanks to another agent, we had pictures of de Chastelain meeting with a member of one of the top crime families in South Carolina. Anyway, I finally cracked his safe open and found the books. There were two sets. One was a record of income from the legitimate side of his import/export business, the second set of books held doctored numbers. That's the income that was reported to the IRS. The other one kept up with what they really brought in. Anyway, by the end of the investigation, the only thing he was able to be charged with was tax evasion." She shook her head, took a sip of her soda. "I had a small microphone planted in his office, but he never mentioned murder, gun running, or the transporting of illegal aliens from Mexico to Texas, then on to South Carolina—at least not in a way that we could pin a charge on him. But he did brag about stealing the IRS blind."

Lucas looked a little green. She placed a hand over his. "Are you all right?"

"I'm not sure. Is there more?"

"Yes."

"How much?"

"Dr. Lucas!"

They turned as one to see the nurse rushing toward them.

Anna's heart stopped. Paulo.

Nurse Lindsey, the woman assigned to Paulo, said breathlessly, "Paulo's in cardiac arrest. They're working on him now."

Anna and Lucas bolted from the cafeteria and took off down the corridor.

Arriving at Paulo's room, they found him surrounded by medical staff but still alive. Machines whirred, Mark barked orders, nurses jumped…and Paulo fought like a trouper.

Anna felt tears clog her throat. How did she pray? If she prayed for a heart for Paulo, she was praying for someone else to die. Shutting her eyes, she told the Lord, *It's in Your hands, God, whatever You decide is best.*

For the next hour, she and Lucas paced and she prayed. Finally, Mark came out to tell them that Paulo was bouncing back and would be in good hands for now but said in all seriousness, "I hope he gets a heart soon. He doesn't have much longer without it." Lucas followed Mark back into the room, leaving Anna to wilt against the wall.

Relief battled grief. Relief that the little boy had pulled through this setback and grief that another person would have to die for Paulo to live.

Then she realized something. And the sudden glaring insight into her character slugged her in the gut, leaving her breathless, nearly gasping out loud. She stumbled to a chair and dropped into it, staring into space, seeing nothing but the past four years of her life.

Then in crystal clarity she saw how hard Paulo fought, pushing through his fear, battling the odds that were against him, conquering one obstacle after another—with faith and courage—and sheer bulldog stubbornness. She'd often thought how brave he was, been amazed at his willingness to never give up, been brought to her knees at his incredible, unconditional love for the God who created him.

But she had never realized what a coward she'd become.

Until now.

And with that same discerning eye, she now saw what she had to do if she ever wanted to be free of the fear that held her captive.

Oh Lord, tell me no. And yet, how can I say I have faith when I live in fear?

One way or another she was going to have to find that evidence. The evidence that she knew was there, some-where in de Chastelain's house. That was why she was here. And, she blew out a breath in disbelief, God had used a sick little boy and a caring doctor, to get her here.

Still stunned at her self-realization and what God was asking her to do, she sat there in a fog of thought trying to decide what she should do first. Where should she start?

The little rush of excitement took her by surprise. Oh, it didn't overpower the all-consuming fear, but it was there—that feeling she used to get before venturing out on a new case. For the next thirty minutes, she sat in the hospital waiting room, praying, formulating a plan. She was going to catch a murderer. After four years, she was going to complete her case.

De Chastelain.

A short phone call later to Justin Michaels, her former supervisor, informed him of her impending arrival. He'd been blown away to hear that she was actually right here in his city and was definitely anxious to talk to her.

Slipping from the room, she planned to catch a cab to the FBI headquarters branch office downtown. Part of her dreaded returning to that place, yet another part of her was anxious to see if revisiting the location where she'd been shot would enable her to put the nightmare to rest.

Only one way to find out.

"Where are you going?"

Lucas's voice startled her. She turned, gulped at the effect he had on her blood pressure, ignored it for the umpteenth time, and said, "I'm going to call a cab. I need to go see my former supervisor, Justin Michaels, and figure out if we can pull together a plan to put de Chastelain away for good—before he gets released."

"I'll go with you. I've got the rental, remember?"

"I can take a cab, and besides, I'd rather you not go."

"Well, too bad. I'm going. Paulo's stable and being carefully monitored. I've got my cell, and the hospital will call if I'm needed. I've got no reason not to go."

"Lucas, that's crazy. I don't even know…I mean…"

"Exactly what are you trying to say, Anna?"

"It could be dangerous and I don't want you involved if I'm putting myself back into the line of fire."

THREE

He stilled, keys swinging from his fingers. "'Back in the line of fire'?"

Anna snapped her mouth shut. *Oh, Lord, he's been my best friend for close to three years. Don't let him do something stupid like think he has to try to help…or stop me from doing what I need to do.* She was well aware the only reason their relationship hadn't gone beyond friendship was because of his attitude toward God…and the fact that she hadn't quite put her past to rest. But she also knew the "more than friendship" feelings were right there waiting to burst forth and make themselves known.

Tucking the keys back in his pocket, he placed his hands on her shoulders, forcing her to look at him. Brown eyes stared down at her. She swallowed hard as he demanded, "Anna, what do you mean, 'back in the line of fire'?"

Tears welled, and she blinked them back. "Four years ago, I was…under special protection." In the hospital recovering from a bullet wound and an emergency hysterectomy while the person who'd shot her got away clean, but she left out those details. "The two FBI agents assigned to guard me…died. They died protecting me, okay? I can't let anyone else get in the way, put themselves in the path of this killer. Especially not you."

His eyes glinted at that last part, but he didn't address it. Instead he asked, "What else is there, Anna? What else were you going to tell me down in the cafeteria before we were interrupted?"

Glancing at her watch, she grimaced. How much should she say? Justin would be waiting for her, but she couldn't just walk out on Lucas. Spying two chairs down the hall, she nodded toward them, talking as they sat. "I knew de Chastelain was into much more than just tax evasion. I couldn't leave it alone. So, I decided to give it one more shot. My 'employer' was still *supposedly* in India. His wife was at a party and the kids were in bed. I went down to his office to do one last search, but I heard a noise in the living room. Thinking one of the children might be up, I went to check it out, but as I got closer, I realized it was voices belonging to several men. No one was supposed to be in that house but me, the kids and the live-in housekeeper who slept on the third floor. Now here were these strange men in the living room and I had two kids to protect. Just as I was about to call 911, I heard some grunts, a yell, harsh breathing. Then I heard, 'Get rid of him.'"

"Oh, Anna…"

"I peeked around the corner to see my employer, obviously not in India, bending over the body holding a knife. He must have flown home that day without letting anyone know. I decided to get out of there. There was no way I could take on all of them and live to tell about it. Backup would take too long. I fled, but must have made some noise because I heard someone coming.

The closest room was his office. I slipped in and hid under the desk."

Lucas shut his eyes as though he couldn't bear the picture she was painting. "When I scrambled under the desk, I heard something. A buzzing noise. It was coming from a little hidden drawer up under the far corner of the desk. I pulled it open and found a BlackBerry. I just knew that this was the evidence we'd been looking for. There was an e-mail waiting to be read—the buzzing sound I'd heard—so I clicked on it. It was asking if the 'deed had been done.' I assumed the 'deed' was the dead body I'd just seen. Anyway, I read enough to know that this could put the man away for a good long time, palmed the memory card, shoved the device back into the drawer and caught my breath. Then the door opened."

Now Lucas looked a little mad. "I can't believe you haven't told me this during the three years we've known each other. What happened?"

Dropping her head to her hands, she muttered through her fingers, "I tried to forget it, Lucas." Looking up, she added, "And it's not like I didn't want to tell you. I just didn't want to relive it. I haven't talked about it in four years. The only person I've had contact with is Justin. And it's not like you've told me every last detail of your life, either." He looked away and she knew she'd scored a direct hit. Hmm…he was hiding his own secrets. She refused to feel bad for not baring her soul. "Anyway, when the door opened, I knew I had to get rid of that card. If he caught me and decided to have me searched, I was dead."

"Anna, that's…"

"I know." She waved him off. She couldn't deal with

the pain, the sympathy, the fear for her that he had written in his eyes. Reciting the details of that night wasn't so difficult as long as she kept an emotional distance from it, as if she were talking about a past case that held nothing personal for her. But if he started showing concern, she'd lose what little control she had over her fear and her emotions. "I've been checking up on him, keeping tabs on the results of our sting, waiting to see if they ever found enough evidence to try him for murder, but just recently Justin said he's on his way out. He told me they never found any other evidence on him and certainly nothing to indicate a murder ever happened."

"So what happened when he opened the door to the office?"

"I had to get rid of the card. There was an umbrella stand right there by the desk, so I dropped it in there."

"Did de Chastelain see you there at the house? Does he know you saw him holding the knife?"

She shook her head. "No way. I realized I'd be next if they knew what I'd seen. I was in shock at the way things had gone down, but thinking clearly. Someone opened the door only seconds after I replaced the Black-Berry into its hiding place. I pretended to be searching for something for one of the children, making a lot of noise, muttering to myself, acting like I was completely unaware of anything else but my search. If questioned, I would explain that I had just tucked the kids in. Andrew couldn't sleep without his pacifier. The reality was I had one in my pocket. So, I pulled it out and tossed it into the corner near the desk.

"Anyway," she continued as Lucas listened intently, "I knew my time to run was short. There were security cameras all over the house. What if one of them caught me standing outside that office door? I didn't have to get the card. I could only hope the books would be enough for a search warrant, which would result in finding the card."

"So, what did you do?"

"I grabbed the books, walked out the front door and took off. I went straight to my supervisor and told them what I saw, that my cover was blown. Because just as soon as de Chastelain checked his BlackBerry and discovered the missing card, I was toast. We threw together a team and got a search warrant, but by the time they raided the house, they found nothing. The card was gone, but de Chastelain was furious with me for turning over his books. I was under FBI protection when someone tried to kill me. Two agents assigned to protect me were killed, I escaped through a fluke, flew off to Brazil. End of story." She didn't bother telling him that she'd been shot coming out of the FBI headquarters and had gotten the rest of the story after she'd awakened from surgery. The words just wouldn't come yet.

"I don't think so."

"Well, it's all you're going to get for now. I need to get going."

"All right, let's go."

Everything about him shouted he was going with her whether she liked it or not. She didn't, but could see she'd have no choice in the matter. Fine, he could come to the meeting…then she'd find a way to ditch him. For his own good.

Anna told Lucas she'd meet him at the car, but had to visit the ladies' room first. Entering the restroom, she walked to the sink to stare at the mirror above it. The room was empty, echoing every sound she made. Her breathing sounded harsh in her ears while her blood thrummed through her veins and her heart beat in rhythm to the pounding in her head.

Dumping those memories in Lucas's lap had felt…freeing somehow. And yet, at the same time, it brought even more clearly into focus her fears, and the turmoil she'd lived with for the past four years rumbled back to the surface, making her into a boiling pot of emotions. She'd needed a moment to get herself together before going to see Justin, because coming face-to-face with her former supervisor was going to bring back even more unpleasant memories. Memories she'd rather leave buried. Unfortunately, that wasn't an option.

Taking a deep breath, she let it out slowly. Hearing the door whoosh open behind her, she scooted into a stall, not wanting to paste on a false smile or look anyone in the eye. Locking the door behind her, she leaned against it, still lost in fighting her reaction to the memories, the fear that wanted to surface and take over.

Footsteps sounded, stopping first in front of the row of sinks, then moving toward the stalls. Her senses tuned in and she stilled, zeroing in on the sound. The steps moved heavily, sounded clunky. Steps like a man might make. She froze, then turned sideways to peer through the crack. Broad shoulders, muscles, definitely a man. She caught a brief glimpse of dark pants, a white shirt. Hiking boots? Then the person entered the stall next to her. Wrong restroom or something more?

Anna shivered, swallowed hard as she acknowledged her only protection right now was a thin metal door. She hadn't wished for a gun in four years. Today, she did. Why was she so nervous? No one knew she was here.

Adrenaline flowed freely as she pondered what to do. Should she call out? Speak? Call Lucas on her cell phone? Justin? Shifting her backpack, she set it on the back of the commode, keeping her eye on the crack in the stall.

Fingers fumbled for the phone.

Hard metal touched the back of her head. She froze. Dropped her purse. Heart pounding, fear exploding, she remembered the feel of a bullet piercing her stomach. The bullet hitting her was memory. The feel of the gun on her skull wasn't. Gritting her teeth, she couldn't do anything about the shaking as she forced the words from her mouth. "What do you want?"

"Go back to Brazil before you get hurt, little girl," a voice rasped in a low whisper from up above. He'd be standing on the toilet, hanging over the wall separating the stalls. "Don't bother calling the police. They won't find me. This is your only warning." With the nose of the gun, he shoved hard, knocking her off balance. Her leg hit the toilet bowl. She missed catching herself and landed on the floor—hard. The door beside her opened, then swung shut. Retreating footsteps, the main door whooshing, then silence—broken only by the sound of her harsh, hiccuping breathing.

Her mind screamed at her to get up and chase him. Don't let him get away with this! But fear had her paralyzed. Nausea swirled. Fortunately she didn't have to go far to lose what little she'd eaten that day.

Then she got mad. Mad at herself for caving in to the fear. Furious at her weakness but still shaking, she opened the stall door and stepped out. Whispering a prayer, she gathered every ounce of courage, strode to the main door and yanked it open. She looked up one hall, then down the other.

Nothing.

At least, no one wearing the clothing she had glimpsed.

Okay, she was back to square one. The whole reason she'd entered the bathroom in the first place. She needed to pull herself together so she could go meet with Justin. And she needed to rinse her mouth. *Lord, I'm going crazy here. How did he know I was here? There's no way anyone can know. Justin is the only one.*

By the time she stepped out of the hospital, after another deep breath, she had herself relatively collected. And she had a few questions for Justin.

Lucas headed to the car to wait for Anna to join him. Shoving his hands in his pockets to protect them against the cold, he made a mental note to purchase a pair of gloves as soon as possible.

Paper crinkled in his palm and he pulled it out to stare at the tract the teen from the airport had given him. The title caught his eye. *God has a plan for your life.* Hmm. Well, so far the plan wasn't exactly working out, in his opinion.

Maybe that's because you haven't given God a chance to direct it.

Whoa. Where had that thought come from? But then he realized it was true. He'd been pushing God away for so long, was it any wonder his life was upside down? Oh, it wasn't terrible. Brazil had been a definite improvement over what he'd left behind, he just felt…incomplete, like something was missing.

Like a relationship with Anna?

Or, more likely, a relationship with God?

"Hey Lucas!"

The shout brought his head around to see Mark coming toward him and he felt a huge sense of relief at the distraction from his thoughts. The smile on the man's face eased his instant worry that something had gone wrong with Paulo again. Mark reached him, saying, "I thought that was you."

"I'm waiting on Anna. What's up?"

"Do you think you'll have any free time in the next couple days?"

Lucas thought. His main purpose for coming home was to be there for Paulo. And to reconcile with his father. No matter how hard he tried to deny it, no matter how much he tried to forget the reason he'd taken off for Brazil three years ago, the past still hurt and he wanted to somehow make it right. He'd be here a while. "Sure, I probably can arrange it, why?"

Mark gave a shrug. "Just thought we could get together for lunch or something, you know, catch up with each other." He gave Lucas a playful punch in the arm. "Hey, man, I've missed you."

And Lucas had missed his best friend. Much more than he'd realized. "Lunch it is. Just name the place and the time."

"Well, it might end up being hospital fare, but at least the company will be interesting."

Offering Mark a grin, he agreed. Then he looked up to see Anna coming his way, beautiful as always…and pale, shaken, like something was wrong. He frowned, reaching for her hand as she approached him. The smile she pushed to her lips for Mark was forced and Lucas squeezed her fingers. She looked up at him. "Are you ready?"

"Ready when you are." He got the message. Questions could wait until later. He nodded to Mark. "Give me a call."

"You got it."

Since their meal at the hospital had been interrupted, Anna and Lucas drove through the nearest Starbucks for bagels and a coffee.

She had called Justin from the hospital to tell him she was running late but on her way. Then she'd told Lucas what happened in the restroom, and he wanted to call the cops. But she convinced him it wouldn't do any good; she wanted to talk to Justin first. Lucas didn't like it, but decided to go along with it—for now. Justin was waiting for her as they walked in the door. He was a tall man, around Lucas's height with a military crew cut and a firm no-nonsense jaw that had felt more than one fist. The large bump in the middle of his nose said it had been broken once upon a time. Green eyes took in Anna's appearance in one sweep, then flared with recognition. "Anna Freeman? You don't look like the Anna I knew four years ago."

"It's me."

"The voice is the same, but…wow. You've changed." He turned to Lucas, sizing him up and seeming to approve of whatever it was he saw. "Is he coming with you? We can talk in front of him?" At Anna's nod, he gestured them into his office, saying, "I would've picked you up at the hospital, you know. In fact, if you hadn't said you were leaving that very minute, I would've insisted."

Lucas clenched his jaw at the man's tone, but he kept quiet. Better to watch and observe first, and act later.

Anna shook her head. "No need." She'd tell him about the restroom incident later.

"So, who's this guy?"

"This is Lucas Bennett. Lucas, meet Justin Michaels."

The men nodded at each other. Lucas and Anna took seats on the ugly green sofa from the nineteen sixties, and Justin sat in the faux-leather chair behind his desk. He looked pointedly at Anna. "You've been gone a long time."

"I've been hiding." In more ways than one. Not just physically, but emotionally, too.

"And you've done it well."

Ignoring every unasked question behind those words, she decided to cut to the chase and said, "I think he knows I'm back." She explained the restroom incident.

Justin frowned. "Not good, my dear. Not good at all. How would he know?"

"I don't know, Justin. You tell me. Did you have a trace on my passport?"

Her former boss flushed, and she said, "That's what I thought. Well, who's to say he doesn't have the same capabilities and has been waiting for me to come back? He knew I came from Brazil. He mentioned it specifically."

Blowing out a breath, Justin shook his head. "It's unlikely, but not impossible."

Anna fisted her hands on her thighs and looked Justin in the eye. "He's going to get away with it, isn't he?"

Justin rubbed his jaw, leaned back and crossed his legs. "Yeah, unfortunately, it looks like he will."

"I want to find the evidence you need to nail this guy. I *saw* him standing over the body holding the knife. The man was bleeding on the floor begging for his life. Then he quit talking. Then they started moving the body, and I hid."

"We searched for it, Anna. The office, the desk, everything. Nada. No secret drawer, no hidden Black-Berry, nothing in the umbrella stand…and no dead body."

"I don't get it. I know I shoved it in there."

"Well, our guys didn't find it. We even confiscated his computer based on the tax stuff and altered books you gave us. Our specialists still came up with nothing."

Anna stood. "No, he wouldn't put anything on his computers. Not even e-mails. I told you that." She sighed. "Then I guess it's over. If you can't find that memory card, I have no way of proving anything. You can't even figure out who the body might have been." She closed her eyes, rubbed her forehead with thumb and forefinger. "Maybe I dreamed it all."

Justin spread his hand in a beseeching manner. "I'm not saying I don't believe you—in fact, just the opposite. The fact that the security camera in that room had been turned off tells me something happened there and de Chastelain planned ahead of time to make sure it wouldn't be caught on tape. The attempt on your life made it obvious someone was out to get you. The deaths of two good agents mean that I believe you saw what you say you saw. I'm saying I just can't prove it. Somehow, I need to get new evidence on this guy and I need it soon."

Anna couldn't pin down the main emotion raging through her right now. She felt fear, anger and disbelief that de Chastelain might actually go free. And part of that was her fault. She should have planted microphones all over the house, not just the office. Clenching her fists, shoving aside the terror at what she was about to say, she stared at Justin and let the words tumble from her lips. "What do I need to do to get back in the game?"

FOUR

Lucas protested, "No way, this is just too dangerous." He looked at Justin. "How could you even think of putting her life in danger again? You couldn't protect her last time and even lost two agents, what makes you think this time would be different?"

Before Justin could respond, Anna placed a calming hand on Lucas's forearm, appreciating his defense of her but aggravated at the same time. "Stay out of this, Lucas. I appreciate that you care, but I didn't ask you to come."

Hurt flickered in his expressive eyes right before a shutter closed off his feelings from her view. "Fine. I'll wait outside while you figure out how to get yourself killed." He left the room without a backward glance.

Blowing out a breath, her heart told her to go after him. Common sense said the sooner he left, the safer he would be. She was trained for this, he wasn't. Mentally, she made another check mark by the category "apologies owed to Lucas" then focused back in on what Justin was saying. "…might need to get you back under our protection."

No way. Not that. "Can you search his house again?" she asked.

"We could if we had probable cause. Unfortunately, I don't have that."

"Then it'll have to be me." Nausea churned at the thought. "I'll have to go back in there and find it."

A surprised snort slipped from his nose. "I don't care how different you look. You'd be recognized in a heartbeat. No way."

"Come on, Justin, even you almost didn't recognize me earlier. And you'll just have to come up with a valid reason to search the man's house again. You and I know his criminal activities didn't stop because he was in jail. As much as I don't want to do this and, honestly, wouldn't have considered it before this morning, I'm determined now, Justin." She leaned back against the plastic sofa, crossing her arms over her stomach. "So we need to come up with a plan."

"Still thinking crazy, aren't you?"

Anna swung around. Lucas stood in the door, one shoulder casually posed against the doorjamb. Her emotions lurched. But fear for him overshadowed anything else. She arched a brow. "I thought you left."

"I'm back now."

Justin broke in, back to business. "Forget it, Anna. It would be suicide. I can't even consider it. You know that. In fact, I should be tossing you into protective custody after that restroom incident."

She bit her lip, thinking hard, examining her emotions. Was there any way in the world she could pull this off without the memories destroying her? She'd gotten herself to the place where she could hold a gun again, but what would happen if she found herself on the wrong end of one? Would she be able to handle it? She insisted, "I'm not going into protective custody. And I want to do this. I *have* to do this."

"No!"

Anna cringed at Lucas's outburst.

Justin shot a look at Lucas, slapped his hands on his desk and rose to his feet. "I'm afraid I agree with your boyfriend here. You've been out of the field a long time. And your cover was blown. I can't even consider sending you back in there." He shook his head. "No, we'll figure something out. Just give me a little time."

How much more time did the man need? She rubbed her left side, moving her hand across her abdomen. It was tempting to give in and assume someone else would take care of everything, but she couldn't take that chance. "So, what now?"

"Lay low. Hide out. We're actually working on something, coming from things at a new angle. If this works, the only thing we'll need you for is when all this comes to trial. So keep your head low and keep in touch, okay? And if anything else happens, you're going into protective custody whether you want to or not."

Not likely, but she ignored that point. "A new angle? What new angle?"

"The wife."

"Oh brother, you'll never get anything out of her. She's as jealous as the day is long, but she's fiercely loyal to the man."

"Well, we've also come back to looking for de Chastelain's brother. It's crazy. There's practically no information on Brandon de Chastelain. As you know, both boys were in the foster care system forty years ago. But we can't find his records anywhere. Back then everything was done on paper. Things got misfiled, lost, whatever. Shawn is all over the place. But Brandon…" He shook his head. "Nothing. All we know is that the two boys were raised in foster care from the time Shawn was six years old. We haven't even managed to find a birthdate for Brandon."

"What *do* you have?"

"I'm getting to that. There's a Brandon de Chastelain somewhere in Canada. We're going on the assumption that's the brother we're looking for. He's a street preacher, of all things. No known address, no credit cards, no bank accounts, you name it. There's nothing even on the Internet about him. He lives on the streets with the people he ministers to. We've been trying to find him for over a year now. We're thinking he moved on to another area, but we're at a loss as to just where to start looking."

Justin was shaking his head, rolling his eyes. "But the brother was a dead end four years ago, so I'm not holding out much hope now. Nevertheless…do I need to put you up in a safe house somewhere or can you stay beneath the radar until we get this wrapped up?"

"You think it's going to happen soon or will I be 'flying beneath the radar' while another four years go by?"

Justin flushed red, the vein in his temple starting to pound.

Anna held up a conciliatory hand, "Sorry, I'm sorry. That was uncalled-for. Although if that guy had wanted to kill me, he would have pulled the trigger. But he didn't, which is a bit strange. Regardless, I will keep out of sight as much as possible. But that doesn't mean I won't be working on digging for more information."

"I'll watch out for her," Lucas promised.

"And you're trained in…what?" Justin asked derisively.

"Well, I'm pretty good with a scalpel, and I'll be staying in a house with better security than Fort Knox."

"You can stay with me," Lucas announced as they left the FBI office, both of them shivering once again in the nippy air. The smell of hot dogs coming from the sidewalk vendor's cart tantalized her nose. Then his statement smacked her brain.

Anna nearly tripped on her way down the steps, his comment registering through the rush of memories that had just assaulted her. She was now standing on the very step where she'd been shot four years ago.

"Excuse me?" she asked.

"I don't mean with me alone, I mean with me…at my father's house, with the rest of my strange extended family and our loyal staff."

Her mind played the mental video she couldn't shake. She could still see the bullet come from the crowded sidewalk, feel the burn as it slammed into her. She swallowed hard and stated absently, "I thought you and your father didn't exactly get along."

"The understatement of the year, but nevertheless, that's where I'm going to stay. Trust me, there's room."

She didn't respond, her mind caught in the vividness of the past. It had been a cold day, with snow dusting the streets. But the weather hadn't stopped the crowd from showing up and protesting the FBI's arrest of one of the city's most prominent businessmen and benefactors. She remembered the precise sound the gun had made as the shot rang out, the exact feel of the bullet as it hit her. Her breathing accelerated as she pictured the person with the gun, ski mask covering features she'd strained to see. The figure melting back into the screaming, scrambling crowd. Then she was falling, falling, everything happening in slow motion as sounds rushed by, voices called her name, then the pain faded and darkness settled over her like a warm blanket on a cold night.

"Anna!"

Blinking, she focused back in on Lucas. The concern in his eyes wrapped itself around her heart. His hands rested on her upper arms, and he'd obviously been calling her name for some time. He gave her another shake. "Are you all right?"

"I…no. I mean, yes. I was just…remembering something."

"Not something pleasant, that's clear. Want to share?"

How did one share the kind of grief that was ripping through her very being, tearing her heart from the depths of her body? What could she say? *God, please help me.*

"No," she said. "I can't stay with you. I mean…I can get a hotel room. It's not a big deal."

His expression said he didn't buy her evasion but was going to let her get away with it. Then he shrugged. "Maybe I want you there for the moral support."

"Oh." He needed moral support? To deal with his family? Obviously there was way more to his past than he'd told her during their talks in Brazil. She eyed him. "I don't think that's a good idea. I can't take the chance that I might put you or your family in danger. Somehow de Chastelain will find out I'm back—if he hasn't already. And when he knows, he'll be after me, mowing down anyone in his path."

Lucas gripped her arm, pulling her to a halt. "Look, Anna, we've been friends for a long time. When you agreed to bring Paulo to America, I can't tell you how relieved I was. I wanted the time with you…was hoping maybe here, we could…" He looked away, seeming to search for the words.

Longing mixed with shock curled through her. He'd come for her. To be with her because he felt the same thing she did. He also knew why neither of them could explore the possibility of a relationship other than friendship. Yet. But his action said he still held out hope…

"I…I don't know what to say. I mean if the circumstances were different…" But they weren't. "Don't you understand? If something happened to you because of me…" Her throat clogged. "I can't take that chance."

"It's not up to you. I'm a big boy. Sure, I'm here for Paulo, but you can count on the fact that I didn't come all the way back to America just to wave goodbye to you and send you on your way to face death all by yourself. I'm in this with you…all the way."

"Lucas…"

Placing a finger over her lips, he shushed her. She gulped as he trailed the finger past her mouth, under her chin, then curved his hand around her neck. He continued. "And I know what you're thinking." Narrowing his eyes, he promised, "If you decide to disappear, I'll hunt you down. I'll haunt the FBI office until someone tells me what I want to know."

"Don't you realize the danger you could be putting yourself in?" Anguish curled in her stomach at the thought of what could happen to him.

He quirked a crooked smile. "Then you'd better keep me with you so you can keep an eye on me."

She stared up at him, her mouth working, but nothing came out. He tapped her chin and her lips came together.

He sighed. "Look, my father suffered a stroke about a year ago. I almost hopped a plane when it happened, but Godfrey, my cousin, told me that it was very mild, nothing the man couldn't bounce back from, so…"

"You stayed in Brazil."

Lucas closed his eyes, raised thumb and forefinger to rub them as though he could erase what lay behind them. "Yeah. I took the coward's way out and let Godfrey handle everything. I kept in touch with him and Father's been fine, recovering nicely. But when I started lining things up for Paulo…it got me to thinking that it was time to see if anything had changed around here." He slid a narrow look in her direction. "And when you agreed to come…"

She ignored the fact that her entire being tingled at his last words. "So, has anything changed?" He was holding something back from her.

"I called Father from the airport and nearly shocked him into another stroke. Godfrey and Dahlia, his wife, have been living there, looking after things for the past nine months or so, ever since he came home from rehab. They're having the staff get our rooms ready."

"You told them I was coming?"

"I told them there was the…possibility…I might be bringing a guest."

"I see." She eyed him, wondering if he'd really put his life on the line just to keep up with her. Yes, he would. But it was the fact that he'd so easily read her mind while she'd been thinking about slipping off and disappearing that really got her. Keeping him with her might be the only way to ensure his safety. She'd give it a trial run and see but knew she'd be looking over both sets of shoulders…his and hers. Throwing her hands up in surrender, she asked, "Okay, do you want to go straight to the house or back to the hospital to check on Paulo?"

"I'll give the hospital a call while we head toward my father's house. If Paulo needs us, they have my cell number."

While Lucas drove and talked with the hospital, Anna made a mental list of what she needed to do. "Flying beneath the radar" wouldn't be possible if she was going to figure out what happened to that evidence she'd found and apparently hid too well. The only plan she could come up with was devising a disguise of some sort to throw them off her trail. She'd think on what kind later. But that would gain her access to the house, then somehow, she'd have to create a diversion, slip into the office and have a look around. She sighed. Who was she kidding? Four years had gone by. Shawn's wife had probably remodeled that house fifty times over by now. The umbrella stand had most likely gone the way of some tax deductible path.

But still…she could look. No harm in that, right?

Glancing in the side mirror, she noticed a fast approaching car coming up behind them. A black car with tinted windows. The Mercedes symbol glinted in the sunlight. Anna blinked at the glare and adjusted the mirror.

"Hey Lucas, you might want to move over into the right lane; that Mercedes is riding awfully close on your bumper."

"You're right. I just noticed that." He signaled, pulled

to the right. The Mercedes followed. Now, Anna became concerned. Lucas sped up, the powerful black car followed easily.

"Lucas, something's not right with this."

No sooner had the words left her lips than the Mercedes gunned it and rammed into the back of the rental.

FIVE

Anna heard Lucas yell and felt herself thrown back against the seat, then bounced off the passenger door. Her head cracked against the window, pain radiating. The seat belt cut into her shoulder and waist, pinning her in the seat. She threw her arms out and grabbed the dash turning to look at Lucas's horrified expression. He wrenched the wheel to the left to avoid a headlong plunge off the highway. Wheels screeched against the pavement, the smell of burned rubber singed her nose.

"Lucas!"

"Hold on!"

The black Mercedes crept up closer, the tinted windows making it impossible to see anything inside. The powerful engine roared. Anna swiveled to look out the back window to get a look at the driver, hoping the front window wouldn't be darkened, but before she could catch a glimpse, the Mercedes gave a sudden burst of speed to ram into the tail end once again. She screamed as the rental went into a tailspin.

Fighting the steering wheel, Lucas growled, focusing his attention on keeping them in the right lane and out of oncoming traffic. Anna grabbed her purse from the floor, searching frantically. She pulled her cell from the side pocket and punched in three numbers.

"Nine-one-one, what's your emergency?"

"We're on Standing Wave Highway heading toward North Carolina. Someone's trying to run us off the road!"

A slight pause. "I have a car on the way. Give me a specific exit number if you can."

"Passing Exit 53. Hurry! Lucas, watch out. They're coming again!"

The impact jerked her head back into the window for the second time; stars danced before her eyes.

"Ma'am, are you there?" Anna focused back on the 911 operator.

"Yes, I...I'm here, but we need some help. Fast."

Lucas managed to dodge another run at the car. The Mercedes slid past, the brake lights flashing. Two more minutes of watching Lucas avoid another collision had her nerves stretched to the breaking point. Finally a siren sounded to her left, another up ahead. The Mercedes immediately backed off, took the next exit and disappeared, but not before Anna thought she caught a glimpse of the number 1 on the license plate. Not that that information would do any good. How many Mercedes would be registered in the city of Rocking Wave Beach with a 1 as one of the numbers on the license plate? It would be like looking for the proverbial needle in a haystack.

Lucas slowed, allowing the police to catch up. One went after the Mercedes, but Anna didn't hold out hope that he would catch it. Her head hurt. Lifting a hand to the throbbing ache centered over her right eye, she felt wetness. When she looked, bright red stained her fingers.

Her door opened and the officer, seeing her blood, said something into his radio. Lucas reached over to grab her left hand. "Are you all right?" he demanded.

She lifted her eyes to his. "So much for staying under the radar, huh?"

How had they found her so fast? Lucas fumed as he thought. First the hospital and now this. He rubbed his shoulder where the seat belt had cut into it. But he ignored his minor aches and pains as he thought.

How was it possible that she'd been located so quickly? Was it truly possible that de Chastelain had the ability to track her passport usage? Or was it something else? Something so obvious, it was scary. It could also be that FBI guy, Justin. He was the only one who'd known Anna was back. Lucas ground his teeth as he paced the den of his father's home.

The old man had yet to put in an appearance. They'd been let in by Ted, who'd gone to get an ice pack for Anna as soon as he'd heard their story. Anna sat on the couch, the ice pack held to her head. She'd downed two ibuprofen pills without complaint. Her pale features worried him, but Anna assured him she was fine, she just needed to lie down. Maddy, one of the household staff, promised him that their rooms would be ready within five minutes.

When they'd finished giving their statements, the officers had tried to convince them to turn around and go back to the hospital, but Anna had refused. Lucas informed them that he was a doctor, promising to keep an eye on her. They quit pushing it. He'd managed to get the little rental car started and they'd finished the remaining ten-minute drive to the Haven, North Carolina, beachfront home located at the top of the man-made cliffs that overlooked the crashing ocean below.

An easy winding path led down to the boathouse where several boats nestled against the pier. The boathouse itself could be seen from the main house and looked like a small stone cottage. Very quaint and very familiar. The sight of it brought pangs of grief for the brother who'd died there, but still it surprised Lucas how good it felt to be home.

They were now ensconced in his father's house where scents from his childhood, the fresh roses from the winter greenhouse, his father's old pipe, and lemon furniture polish washed over him, reminding him of good days when his mother was alive and he felt loved, sheltered.

"Lucas?"

Spinning on his heel, Lucas found himself face-to-face with the cousin he'd grown up with. His best friend and co-troublemaker. "Godfrey."

Sincere affection flooded him as he crossed the room to hug the man who hadn't aged a bit in the past three years. His dark good looks had always driven girls nuts and he'd reveled in his popularity. Until he'd met Dahlia, now his wife, and was smitten for life. "You look great. It's good to see you."

Godfrey smiled, his blue eyes crinkling at the corners as he patted Lucas's shoulder. "I can say the same for you. Brazil must have been some kind of vacation."

Lucas gave the man a light punch to his shoulder. "Funny." He pushed aside the reason he'd gone to Brazil and said, "Now come here and let me introduce you to a friend of mine. This is Anna Freeman. We met in Brazil at the orphanage, but she grew up just a couple of hours from here in Rocking Wave Beach."

Rising from the couch, Anna held the ice pack in her left hand to grasp Godfrey's outstretched hand with her right. She smiled, but the purple bruise peeking through her wispy blond bangs made her look fragile, like she could be snapped in two without much effort.

Concern gripped Lucas. She really needed to lie down.

Godfrey's eyebrows rose as he spotted her; a frown creased his forehead as he said, "Very nice to meet you. What happened to your head?"

"Someone tried to run us off the road on the way over here."

"Run you off the road!" Godfrey's eyes flew to Lucas. "Why would someone do that?"

"It's…a long story."

"One I think I might like to hear." The clipped voice came from the doorway. "Hello, Lucas. It's been a while, hasn't it?" The three turned to watch the old man enter the room, his dignity worn like a suit of armor. Everything about him shouted money, control, power. His gray hair didn't dare move as it sat upon his round head. The hand on his hip, while aged with spots and wrinkled skin, wouldn't think about giving a betraying tremble.

Looking into his eyes, Lucas realized they were his own. He knew exactly how he would look in thirty years. The man moved stiffly yet regally to stand before Lucas, all signs of a stroke carefully hidden. Even his words were crisp; no slurred speech in evidence, although he spoke slowly, in a deliberate way that Lucas didn't remember from before. "So, the prodigal returns. Shall we kill the fatted calf?"

Lucas swallowed hard. He hadn't realized how he would feel actually seeing the man face-to-face. He felt…he didn't know how he felt…weird. As usual when he felt uncomfortable, he reverted to sarcasm. "The Bible, Father? Did you get religion?"

"Religion? I daresay, not in this lifetime. It was merely an expression. Welcome home, Lucas. It's about time you came back to reclaim your rightful place in the family. I do hope you've managed to, shall we say, sow all your wild oats, and are ready to settle down. I'm quite ready for grandchildren and have a perfectly suitable woman picked out for you."

Between the throbbing in her head and the way her eyes were ping-ponging back and forth between father and son, Anna thought she might very well be on her way to her first migraine ever. *This* was Lucas's father? This stiff, unyielding block of…cement? She shuddered. No wonder Lucas had escaped to Brazil. Why on earth had he come back to this house?

"Excuse me, sir?" said a timid voice above the commotion. "I've got the rooms ready if Mr. Lucas and Miss Anna would like to retire to them."

"Good. That will be all." The man never turned to address the woman. Anna knew some of the upper crust didn't acknowledge their help and that it was perfectly acceptable in some circles. She thought it was just downright rude.

Stepping around Godfrey to offer the woman a warm smile, she said, "Yes, thank you so much for getting it ready."

A hesitant yet appreciative smile slipped across the young woman's face. Anna thought she looked to be about her own age or maybe a couple of years younger. Black curls were pulled back into a ponytail. Anna almost waited for her to offer a curtsy before leaving. Instead, she flashed another smile and an audacious wink that had Anna biting her lip to keep from chuckling.

Lucas said, "Thanks, Maddy. It's good to see you're still here. We'll be right up. I know Anna probably wants to lie down after our little incident." He turned to Anna. "Father, I was just making introductions. Anna, this is my father, Thomas Bennett."

Anna once again held out her hand. The man's hesitation was so scant it was barely noticeable, but Anna caught it. In too much pain to worry about it right now or even feel offended, she just longed to crash onto her bed. She'd worry about finding other living arrangements in a few hours. Judging by the undercurrents and tension emanating from the room, she had a feeling these accommodations weren't going to work out.

"Very nice to meet you, sir. I appreciate your hospitality in allowing me to stay in your home."

"Wasn't really given a choice, but I suppose you're welcome."

Tell me what you really think. Anna zipped her lips tight and stretched them into a closed smile so the words would stay in her mind and not pass her lips. Better to bite her tongue than say something that would later come back to haunt her. Instead she managed, "I'll just be in my room. Thanks."

"This way, miss." Maddy had ignored her earlier dismissal from the older man and was waiting for Anna, who followed the woman up the curving stairs, down the wood-paneled hallway to the last door on the right. "Here you are, miss."

"My name's Anna. May I call you Maddy?"

"Of course. You're a guest. You may call me anything you like."

"Well, we'll see how long I last as a guest." Not long, most likely. She was going to have to leave at the first opportunity. Her pounding head told her that would be right after a nap and most likely some more ibuprofen.

Maddy giggled then slapped a hand over her mouth. "Sorry, but I like you."

Anna grinned through her weariness. She definitely needed to lie down, her tongue was loosening. "Thanks, Maddy. I can take it from here."

"I'll be right back with your bags."

"Normally, I would insist I could get my own bags, but right now I'm going to take you up on it."

"I'll get them," Lucas said from behind. Maddy nodded and left.

Lucas pointed to the box on the wall beside the door. "If you need anything, just buzz Maddy. One security feature that might let you rest a little easier is the red and the green buttons. If you push them, you'll send a silent alarm to the police that we've got an intruder. I doubt you'll need them, but I want you to see just how good the security is around here." Anna nodded her thanks, then grimaced as her head pounded in protest.

Sympathy oozing, Lucas said, "You lie down, I'll get your things."

After he left, Anna took in the beautifully decorated room, noticing the finely carved sculpture in the corner next to the expensive leather love seat. But the thing she wanted most was set back in a small alcove. The queen-size bed with the rose-patterned comforter. Within a minute, she lay stretched across it, ignoring the throbbing in her head, hoping the medicine would kick in soon.

Unable to sleep until the pain lessened, she decided to put the time to good use and think as best she could around her headache. Obviously, getting into de Chastelain's house as an au pair was now out of the question. Somehow, someone had seen her, recognized her and reported her whereabouts to Mr. Shawn de Chastelain, who'd just tried to take her out—and hadn't cared that she was with an innocent person.

Unfortunately, she had a feeling the FBI had a snitch—one named Justin Michaels. The thought was like a kick in the stomach. Her heart ached with the thought that the one person in America she had thought she could trust would betray her. But as she thought about it, she realized he would have had the perfect opportunity. Four years ago, he could have been the one to alert the shooter to the fact that she was at the FBI office and would be leaving…a wide-open target. When she'd awakened from the surgery necessary to remove the bullet, she'd been told she'd never be able to have children thanks to an emergency hysterectomy. All because of one Shawn de Chastelain and his evildoing cohorts.

And today, only a short while after she'd been in contact with Justin, someone had warned her to leave, then tried to kill her when she didn't. Whoever it was knew her moves. The thought chilled her. *Oh Justin, please tell me it's not you. I don't want to believe you could do that. What reason would you have?*

Talking to the man in her head was getting her no answers. All she knew right now was she'd better be watching her back. When fear tried to crowd out reasonable thought, she gave it a good shove and recited the verse that had become her strength. "For God has not given me a spirit of fear…" Slowly her breathing eased.

So now she tried to form a plan. She had to find another way to get in that house—and do it in disguise. But how? The pounding in her head eased and her eyelids drooped. The adrenaline rush was gone, leaving her limp with exhaustion. She closed her eyes on a prayer for God to work through everything, for Paulo to get a new heart and be a healthy little boy, to find the evidence needed to put Shawn de Chastelain in prison where he couldn't hurt any more innocent people and for reconciliation between Lucas and his father. *Oh, and could You give me an extra dose of patience, God? I think dealing with Lucas's father is going to require a bit more than normal—okay, probably a lot more. Guard my tongue, please, Jesus.* "Let the words of my mouth and the meditations of my heart be acceptable in Thy sight, oh Lord, my strength and my Redeemer."

Two hours later, Lucas had showered and checked his e-mail, and would soon be on his way to check on Paulo, but first he stopped by Anna's room to knock softly. When she didn't answer, he peeked around the door to see her stretched out across the bed. Good, she was asleep. Shutting the door gently, he backed away. He'd called the hospital and Mark had reported that Paulo was still hanging in there, his blood work completed. All they needed now was the donor. It bothered him that someone had to die for the little boy to get the heart, but unfortunately that was life—which often involved death.

"Lucas, how is she?"

Godfrey came from the opposite end of the hall where he and Dahlia shared a suite of rooms.

"She's asleep right now. I'm going to head to the hospital to check up on Paulo. Mark said he was doing all right, but I'll feel better if I go over there to see for myself."

"How long do you plan to stay…here, I mean, at the house?"

Lucas shrugged. "I don't really have a timetable in mind. Right now, my goal is to make sure Paulo gets the help he needs, then possibly head back to Brazil." But only if that was where Anna was headed.

"Really?" Godfrey looked surprised then he smirked. "You think you'll go back? I thought you might have 'sown all your wild oats' and would be ready to settle down and raise a few kids."

"Very funny. Since when did you start quoting my father? I've always wanted children but that's no reason to rush the experience…especially with the wrong woman. I have to admit I'm a little shocked at the reception I got from my father. I wouldn't call it warm, but he didn't decimate me. You know he's always blamed me for Lance's death."

His cousin looked away. "Yeah, I know."

"Do you? Blame me, I mean."

"No, Lance was slowly self-destructing. You're just lucky you weren't in the boathouse with him when it exploded."

"Lucky? I don't know. Maybe my father was right. Maybe it should have been me who died instead of Lance."

"Who's Lance?"

Anna's soft question interrupted the cousins' conversation. Godfrey and Lucas's eyes met then Lucas said, "Hey there. I brought your bags up. We didn't mean to wake you."

"You didn't. My stomach did. I'm starving."

Godfrey intervened. "Dinner is served at six-thirty sharp. If you don't want to eat here, I can let the cook know. Or if you do, she always makes enough, so even last-minute decisions one way or another don't really matter."

Lucas looked at Anna and said, "I want to go to the hospital to check up on Paulo. I thought you might not feel well enough to go. You want to stay here or go with me?"

Godfrey's cell phone rang, and he excused himself to answer it. "I want to go see Paulo, but—" she chewed her lip "—I'm afraid of putting him in danger."

"I'll be careful. We'll watch our tail and keep to the main roads. Hopefully, they won't try anything again today. I called your buddy Justin and let him in on what happened. He said they'd send someone to guard Paulo's room if we thought he needed it."

"He did?" She wondered if she should voice her suspicions about her former supervisor. "What else did he say?"

"To be careful and that he'd look into everything."

Deciding to keep her thoughts about Justin to herself for the time being, she said, "All right. Just give me a minute to freshen up."

Anna disappeared back into the room, and Lucas went downstairs to wait just inside the front door for her. When she appeared only moments later, he took a deep breath as he registered just how beautiful she was— even with the nasty-looking goose egg on her forehead.

"How's the head?"

"I'll live. The medicine helped, but I'll need a couple more in an hour or so."

Wrapping an arm around her shoulders, Lucas led her out into the chilly darkness. His eyes darted into the shadows, the hit-and-run incident still fresh in his mind, causing his nerves to jump under his skin. The sun had disappeared about thirty minutes ago, taking every ounce of warmth with it. Anna had on a long-sleeved T-shirt, jeans and tennis shoes along with a light jacket that he hoped would be warm enough. The air smelled like snow, but wasn't cold enough for it even though it sure felt like it. In the distance, he heard the waves crashing against the shore and, with a pang, realized he'd missed his home over the past years.

Since the rental car had been towed off, Lucas had his father's chauffeur pull one of the cars around from the garage. The late-sixty-something man stepped out of the silver Jaguar and handed Lucas the keys. "Thanks, Ted."

"Have a good evening, sir."

Anna slid into the passenger seat and sighed. Lucas had forgotten what a luxury it was to drive such a nice vehicle and nearly went into culture shock. The scent of rich, leather seats filled his nose and the quiet engine purred, whispering the promise of a sweet, smooth ride.

Anna asked, "Does Ted live here, too?"

"Yes. He's been with my family since I was in the third grade. He and his wife, Joni, live in one of the cottages down by the beach. Their children are grown and gone and Ted could retire anytime, but he insists on staying with my father. At least that's the story as of three years ago. I'm assuming it's still true."

"Nice."

"Very. They're good people, you'd like them. They've been trying to get my father to come to church with them for years. You'd think they'd have given up by now."

"Why don't you go to church, Lucas? Every time the subject of God comes up, you run away."

He stiffened, not wanting the conversation to go down that road. "I don't run away. I just don't believe God cares."

"Why? What would make you think that?"

"Come on, Anna, look around you. All the suffering, the pain, the prayers for help that go unanswered. Look at little Paulo in the hospital, waiting for a new heart. Tell me the God you serve cares about all that. And if He does, then why doesn't He do something about it?" The words tumbled from his lips faster than he could keep up with them. But once said, he felt relief. Glad he finally blurted out his true feelings about the subject. He'd never been that blunt about it before. But this was Anna, he could tell her anything.

"Oh, Lucas." She placed a hand on his right arm, and he slid his hand from the wheel to grip her fingers. "I'm so sorry you see it that way. And I'll be honest, I don't have all the answers. Unfortunately, it's not a perfect world. When sin entered it, so did all the pain and misery you're describing. But, God promises to be there during the hard times, and I know from personal experience that He is. I can't always explain it, I just know that even when I'm feeling at my lowest, if I praise His name anyway, I get peace."

"I wish I could understand that."

She gave his hand one last squeeze. "The only way is to give Him a try."

"Yeah." He changed the subject as he made a right turn into the hospital parking lot. "Here we are—and without incident. Let's go check on Paulo."

Anna climbed from the car, her heart rejoicing at the conversation Lucas just initiated. *Please, Jesus, don't give up on him. Keep working on his heart. Show him Your unconditional love. He's never seen it, doesn't understand it, so just show him…somehow.*

As they strode through the lobby, Anna looked at each face she passed, suspicion bubbling through every cell of her body. Would her attacker show up here again? Even the workers putting up the Christmas tree in front of the bay window were suspect; she inspected the two men running the lights around the ceiling and the one woman hanging the mistletoe over her chair. Anna smiled and nodded and took note of the smallest details. Lucas ran into Mark coming out of the restroom and stopped to talk to him.

Anna said, "I'm going to make a quick call, then head up to see Paulo, if that's all right." She looked at Lucas. "You can fill me in on everything later."

"Sure." Lucas waved her on.

Anna headed for the elevator, stepped on and pressed the button for the third floor. As the doors slid shut, a hand reached in at the last moment to shove them open. A man with dark sunglasses stood there staring at her for a brief moment before stepping toward her.

SIX

Anna sucked in a deep breath, immediately suspicious after the recent incident in the restroom, not to mention almost being run off the road. She moved to the edge of the elevator, keeping one eye on the man as he said nothing, just stepped in and turned to face the still open doors.

Dressed in khaki slacks and a long-sleeved dress shirt, unbuttoned at the neck, his broad shoulders and confident carriage shouted purpose, but it was the sunglasses covering his eyes that really creeped her out. Fear flickered in her midsection. She pressed a hand to it, cutting her eyes for a sideways glance at his face.

The man's hand reached up, a finger pointed…and he pressed the button for the fourth floor. Her breath whooshed out silently through pursed lips. You're being paranoid, she told herself, definitely losing it.

He turned to look at her, adjusted his sunglasses, twin dark lenses reflecting her face.

The doors started their smooth glide shut. He pushed his right hand into his blazer…

He's got a gun! Get out, get out, get out, her brain shouted. Beyond caring whether or not she looked like an idiot, she stepped toward the doors, but just as she was about to slip out, an elderly couple rushed on, causing the doors to slide back open, and Anna to move back out of the way. The balding man smiled and said, "Sixth floor, please."

The dark-headed man turned away. Slowly, he pulled his hand from his jacket, nodded to the two newcomers and did as requested. Then he stepped off the elevator. Her breathing slowed. Her pulse stopped galloping and she rubbed her sweaty palms on her jeans. Just because he put his hand in his coat doesn't mean he had a gun, right? Finally, the elevator slid to a stop on the third floor. Anna stepped out on still shaky legs, waited for the door to shut behind her, then turned down the hall to head toward Paulo's room.

Unable to put it off any longer, she pulled out her cell phone and punched in Justin's number. He answered on the third ring.

She got straight to the point. "Are you trying to set me up?"

"What?"

"Justin, who else knew I'd be here? Who else knew what car I'd be in? I don't want to believe it, but I don't know what to think. Every time I run it around in my head, I come up with you. You had a trace on my passport. You probably knew I was back before I did! You could have easily set me up."

Silence filtered through the line. "Thanks a lot, Anna."

A world of hurt loaded down those four little words. She almost felt like weeping. And yet... "I'm sorry, Justin, but you're the only link."

"I don't know what to tell you except I only want to

help you." Anna winced at the pause. Then Justin said, "I promise you this, I'd never do anything to hurt you."

"Yeah." She bit her lip, thought about everything. "Okay, it's just that things started going crazy as soon as I landed on American soil."

"And I'm going to help you figure out why. But I promise, it's *not* me."

"I want to believe that, I really do," she whispered.

A long pause. Then, "Will you accept my help? Let me send someone to keep an eye on you and the little guy at the hospital? Put you under protection?"

"Not a chance. But if something happens to Paulo and I find out you're behind it, I'll hunt you down, Justin." She hung up the phone, grief nearly sending her to her knees. She couldn't believe Justin was behind this, she just couldn't.

Arriving at the right room, she shoved off the lingering fear from her elevator scare and the worry that Justin had something to do with the attempts on her life. Drawing in a calming breath, she gently pushed the door open to see Paulo breathlessly laughing at something Andy had said. Somehow the two of them were managing to communicate in spite of the language barrier. Paulo had picked up a lot of English at the orphanage. He'd even known some before he'd arrived on their doorstep in Tefe.

In just the few hours since he'd been in this hospital, he'd gained a little color. Yes, he still looked tired and weak, but his eyes were shining. When he saw her, he grinned. In his raspy, labored voice, he said, "Miss Anna. I have a new friend. This is Andy. His mom went downstairs to get something to drink. Senhorita Ella went to the restroom."

Crossing to his side, she clasped his small hand then glanced at the boy in the other bed. "Hello, Andy. It's good to see you again. How are you feeling? Better?"

"Yes, but getting tired again."

Paulo rasped, "Yes, me, too."

Sadness gripped her. If she could rip out her own heart and put it into that little body, she'd do it. The fierce love that swept over her rocked her to her very soul and she knew Paulo had become the son she'd never have. She thought about the elevator incident. Was she putting Paulo in danger by being here?

Sure, it's possible she'd been paranoid this time, but that didn't mean next time it wouldn't be the real deal. Sadly, Anna realized that this may have to be her last visit with the little guy depending on how things went in her investigation. She'd just have to make the decision of whether or not to visit a daily judgment. There was no way she was leading anyone anywhere near this child. She choked back the sudden surge of tears, forcing a smile as she leaned over to kiss his silky black curls. "I know, but soon you will be running and playing and building snowmen in the snow."

"Christmas. The day Jesus was born, *sim?* A very special day. You told me all about it, remember?"

"I sure do." And she did. About six months ago, when Paulo had been sick with the virus that damaged his heart, she'd sat by his bed, reading the story of Christ's birth from Luke chapter two. He'd been fascinated with the fact that Jesus was really God but came down as a baby to save the world. She'd read the story so many times over the course of his illness, she could practically quote it now.

"What do you want for Christmas, Paulo? Something special?"

Andy piped in. "I know what I want. I want an Xbox."

Paulo studied Anna's features very seriously before saying, "I do not know. But I will think on it." His eyes fluttered closed. Anna waited, thinking he'd fallen asleep, but then very faintly, she heard, "Sing for me, Miss Anna. The praising song."

Anna blinked. The praising song? Then she remembered. The song she'd sung for him a couple of times while he'd been lying in the hospital. She'd translated it into Portuguese and he'd seemed to relax each time he heard it. "English or Portuguese?"

"English," he whispered, "so Andy can understand the words, too."

So, she held his hand and sang, "'Your name is blessed in all the land, your beauty unsurpassed, your faithfulness never ending. I call on you as I praise your name…" Closing her eyes, she let the words wash over her, opened her entire being to the worship. That indescribable feeling filling her heart, her very soul, with the peace she could only find in her Lord. His presence flooded her, joy nearly choking her as her eyes filled with tears "…you find me when I'm lost, wandering through the darkness, flailing to find You when I can't see…I turn to you praising your name…"

Lucas stood in the doorway to Paulo's room, watching the most beautiful—and unbelievable—thing he'd ever seen. Anna sang in a sweet perfect pitch, praising her God. He listened to the lyrics as she sang about the path she traveled, blessing God's name even in the midst of her torment.

How? How could she do that? What kind of God did

she serve that allowed her to feel the peace that practically oozed from her every pore when it seemed like everything in life was going wrong? Paulo slept as she sang. Andy's eyes were heavy, drooping, fluttering open, then closed.

Stuck, Lucas felt like an intruder on such a private moment. He wanted to leave yet felt compelled to stay. He wanted to kneel down beside her and share in her worship. He wanted what she had.

Her voice filled the small room but there was no mistaking that Anna wasn't there. She was somewhere with her God, the one she worshipped, had faith in and trusted unwaveringly to get her through the hard times.

Lucas felt the presence behind him and jerked around, his finger to his lips. It was Lindsey, the nurse. He wondered how long she'd been there but then realized, from the tears standing in her eyes, she'd been there long enough.

And then there was quiet.

A soothing stillness that made him want to savor every blessed moment.

"Oh, hi," Anna said, her words a little breathless. Seeing her audience, she seemed flustered. "Um, Paulo wanted me to sing to him."

Lindsey sniffed. "Whoo, girl, that was beautiful. Better than any church worship service I've ever been in."

Anna swiped at her face then reached to grab a tissue from the box beside Paulo's bed. Giving a chuckle, she said, "God shows up at the weirdest times and sometimes the strangest ways. I'd planned to just sing for Paulo, and, instead, I ended up singing for Him. I love it when that happens." She giggled again. Lucas wondered at the joy that lingered, the aura of peace that still surrounded her. If he thought he could have that…

"How's Paulo?"

Glancing back at the small boy in the bed, she shrugged. "I think he feels a little better. He had some color in his cheeks when I walked in a little while ago, but he got tired real fast. Andy, too."

"You two need to get on home." Lindsay shooed them off. "It's getting late. Don't you worry, I'll be keeping a close eye on these two all night long."

Footsteps sounded behind him and he turned to see Mark Priestly coming toward him. "Hey there, how's it going?" The serious expression on his face sobered Lucas. "What is it?"

"Paulo just moved into the number-one spot for a heart."

Which meant the person previously in the number one spot had just passed away. Pressing his lips tight, Lucas gave a short nod and Mark turned on his heel to head back down the hall. Probably to talk to the family of the deceased.

Lucas looked at Anna. "Are you ready?"

"I feel I should stay with him." Sorrow darkened her eyes; she'd heard Mark.

"He'll be fine. Ella will be here and Lindsey will call if we're needed. And you need to get some proper rest or your head isn't going to feel good tomorrow."

She lifted a hand to her wound. "I'd forgotten all about it, but now it's starting to throb again. Okay. You're right. Let's go."

First thing the next morning, Anna came downstairs to the smell of breakfast. Scrambled eggs, toast, ham, bacon, orange juice, fresh strawberries and toasted bagels. Her mouth watered as she followed her nose into the dining area. Lucas, already seated with Godfrey across the table from him, looked up when she entered the room. "Good morning," he said.

He stood and pulled out a chair next to him. She stepped past him, and he placed a hand at the small of her back, causing shivers to chase up her spine. Mentally, she fussed at herself for her attraction. She looked around to distract herself and her eyes landed on the petite blonde next to Godfrey. She assumed she was his wife, Dahlia. Anna hadn't met her yesterday as the woman had been otherwise occupied.

"Good morning. I hope I'm not too late."

"I told Maddy to let you sleep in as late as you could. How's your head feeling?"

"It's fine, *Doctor,*" she teased as she sat. Actually, it still ached a little, but nothing she couldn't deal with.

"Anna, this is Godfrey's wife, Dahlia. I've told you a little about her, but I don't think I mentioned she's the president of her own company now. She started Scents of Beauty, a cosmetics company, about six months ago and it's already doing quite well."

"With my help, of course," Godfrey chimed in with a smile. "I've got the business head and Dahlia has the product smarts."

Anna greeted the pretty woman. "Hi, nice to meet you. And congratulations on your success."

"Thank you." Dahlia flashed a smile that didn't quite reach her eyes as she dipped her knife in the butter and made the act of spreading it on her toast an exercise in elegance. She seemed sad, possibly depressed. Anna would certainly recognize the symptoms if she had enough time to analyze the woman. Giving a mental shrug, she decided maybe she was wrong and Dahlia was just reserved. Anna would have to give it time to get to know the woman a little better before making a judgment.

Serving herself, Anna listened to the conversation around her. "So you design fragrances and the like?"

Dahlia looked up at Anna as though surprised at her interest. "Yes," she said slowly, "and a line of makeup that cleanses your skin even as it covers up the flaws."

"That sounds fascinating. How did you come up with the idea?"

A spark of animation flashed in those dark, pretty eyes and a genuine smile lit her features. Wow. No wonder Godfrey had fallen for this woman. Her smile revealed dimples a mile deep. "Oh, I have a Ph.D. in chemistry, and I love makeup. It was a natural fit."

Anna nearly choked on the last bite of eggs she'd just put in her mouth. Okay, she wouldn't have guessed that one. "I'd love to see some of your products."

Before Dahlia could answer, Thomas Bennett entered the room. Conversation immediately ceased and Dahlia's expression closed up just as quickly. He walked stiffly over to the end chair to seat himself without a word of greeting. Since no one seemed inclined to speak, Anna took the initiative. "Good morning, Mr. Bennett."

"What's so good about it?"

Anna bit her lip. Had she made a faux pas? Lucas looked amused. She quirked a brow at him in silent communication. He shrugged.

"Well," she drawled in answer to the man's sarcasm, "it's a beautiful day, and I'm alive to see it. That makes it a pretty good morning in my opinion."

"Humph."

Anna took another bite of egg and vowed to find a different place to stay—soon. She had enough stress in her life without adding to it.

"So, Anna is it?" the man asked haughtily.

"Oh, come off it, Father, you know the woman's name." Lucas shot his father a disgusted look. "Just ignore him, Anna. It's an intimidation tactic, although why he feels the need to intimidate you, I've no idea."

Anna cleared her throat. "Yes, it's Anna."

"Who is your family?"

"Excuse me?"

"Your family? Are you from around here?"

"I was born in Rocking Wave Beach, the only child of only children." She wasn't sure exactly what the man was after.

"And where did you go to school?"

"I went to Rocking Wave High then went to UCLA on a full academic scholarship and majored in Criminal Justice."

"Really?" The look on his face said he was decidedly unimpressed. Anna refused to feel unworthy. Public school didn't measure up in his eyes, no doubt. And she definitely wasn't an Ivy Leaguer, though UCLA would impress most people.

"Yes, sir, really." She took several bites of egg and drank a cup of juice before Lucas stood, determined to put an end to the awkwardness.

"Anna, why don't you bring a biscuit with you? I thought we'd take one of the boats out on the ocean."

Godfrey looked startled. "A boat?"

"Yes, why? Is that a problem?"

"Um…er…no, it's just…after…well…" Godfrey

trailed off, his eyes on Thomas, who now studied his food as though it contained the answers to every question he'd ever had.

Anna wondered at the sudden undercurrents. She flashed a questioning look to Lucas, who reached out and took her hand. He said to Godfrey, "It's all right. It'll be good therapy for me. Facing my past and all that."

"What about Paulo?" Anna asked, concerned the boy might need her there, although, Lucas's comment about facing his past piqued her interest.

"I called about thirty minutes ago to check on him. Ella said that he ate a little breakfast and is looking forward to our visit, but for now, I want to show you something."

Waving goodbye to her breakfast companions, she followed Lucas from the dining area out into the foyer. "What are we doing?"

"I want to take a boat ride."

"I got that part. The question is, why?"

"I'll explain in a minute. Grab your jacket."

Anna did as requested and, within minutes, they were walking down the path that led to the boathouse. As they neared the building, Lucas's steps faltered for a brief moment before he squared his shoulders as though approaching the boathouse equaled going into battle. "Lucas, could I ask you a question?"

"Sure," he said, but he never looked at her, just kept his eyes on the door to the boathouse.

"What's the deal with you and your father? Why is it so tense and formal between you guys?"

"Because I killed my brother."

SEVEN

He blamed himself for Lance's death. As did their father.

"Excuse me?" She stepped in front of him, placing a hand in the middle of his chest to halt his forward progress. "You can't just drop that bomb and walk on. Explanation, please?"

Stopping before the door to the boathouse, Lucas felt the warmth of her hand through his shirt as he'd neglected to zip his coat. It distracted him just a bit, but he kept his focus on the door to the boathouse. Anna waved her other hand in front of his eyes. "Hello?"

"Three and a half years ago my brother and I were supposed to go out with Godfrey to a football game." Anna fell silent and let him talk. He appreciated the gesture while taking in her concern. She was so beautiful, he wanted to…but not now. Gathering the memories in his mind, he decided it was time to face them…and settle them, once and for all, then maybe he and Anna… "Lance was quite a guy, the laid-back, carefree type. But he knew how to work our old man, stay in his good graces. Lance never let on the struggles he was facing…at least not until he started asking me for money."

"What kind of struggles?"

"He was big into the party scene, he and Godfrey. Because of the Bennett name, they rolled with some of the big-shot celebrities, rock stars, politicians. You name it. If there was an invite, he was there. As a result, he got into drugs, alcohol, the whole nasty bit. Godfrey did, too, for a while there but cleaned himself up before Lance died."

"But not you?"

"No." He shrugged. "That kind of thing just never appealed to me. I sometimes went to the parties to keep Lance out of trouble, but overall, with med school and working to make it on my own, I never really had the time for it, even if I'd been interested."

"Why did Godfrey react so strongly to you mentioning the boathouse?"

"Because this is where my brother was killed."

Swallowing hard, she looked at the beautiful stone structure with navy-blue shingles. It looked so peaceful that trying to picture a death happening here seemed… wrong. "Oh. So, what happened?"

"Lance called me that night, asking to meet me here. He wouldn't tell me why, but I could tell he was either drunk or high. I called Godfrey and told him that Lance and I wouldn't be making the ball game. Godfrey was fine with that and I met Lance. He wanted money, of course. He'd gone through his entire month's allowance—which wasn't skimpy—and wanted me to give him more. He knew better than to go to our father. Father would have made him give an accounting of every penny."

"Did you give him the money?"

"No—" he sucked in a deep breath "—and there's

my quandary. I know he wanted the money for more drugs. If I'd given him the money, he might possibly still be alive although most likely still hooked on drugs. But at least he would be breathing, still have a chance to clean himself up. But because I didn't, he's dead."

The memories surged one over the other like the waves beyond the dock. He quit fighting them and let them fill his mind. He told her the story as he relived it. "Lance was quite the smoker. He knew I hated it so I'm sure he lit up for my sake. To goad me, no doubt. You'd think he would have tried to brownnose me or something since he was asking for money. But not Lance. Oh, no. He had too much pride for that. I tried to talk him into going into rehab for his drug addiction, but he wouldn't have any part of it. He said some pretty nasty, hurtful things and I stormed out in disgust, told him to get it together or I'd tell Father what he was really doing with his money. This infuriated him and I'm sure that, as he was spewing his filth, the cigarette fell from his mouth. The investigators said it must have fallen into an open can of gasoline. I'm not sure I buy that, but since no one can know for sure what really happened, I guess it's as good an explanation as any. Anyway, one small explosion let to another and…" He shrugged, his shoulders slumped, losing their normally straight stance as though weighted down with a ton of bricks.

"I was about twenty feet outside the building when I heard a pop. Then the building just seemed to go. Ka-boom." He finished the last word on a whisper, his mind's eye seeing the building burning, the flames reaching for the black blanket of sky above them.

The hand on his arm brought him back to the present, to Anna and the newly built boathouse. Rebuilt to honor

Lance's memory. It had been Lance's favorite place, his haven. Their father had had it reconstructed exactly as it had been, as though the fire had never happened.

Unfortunately, Lucas knew better.

"It wasn't your fault." Her murmured whisper soothed his aching heart.

"My mind knows that, but deep down, I can't help but wonder, what if I hadn't threatened to tell Father? What if I hadn't lost my temper and stormed out? What if…"

"The what-ifs will never lose their grip, Lucas."

"Is that where God comes in?"

She gave a sad smile. "Only if you let Him."

"I want to. I know sometimes I give you a hard time or act cynical, but…" He stuck a hand into his coat pocket and pulled out a small rectangular piece of paper. "I read this. A girl gave it to me in the airport."

Curiosity flickered and she asked, "What is it?"

"A tract."

Joy flared on her face. "And you kept it? I would have thought you'd have given it a toss at first opportunity."

"I almost did but then forgot about it until last night. I pulled it out of my pocket to throw it away. Instead I started reading it."

"And?"

He pursed his lips. "And…I need to think about it some more."

The disappointment flashed only briefly before she nodded. "Sure, just let me know when you want to talk."

He took a deep breath and forced a smile. "Absolutely. Now, do you want to go for a boat ride?"

* * *

Over the course of the week, this became their morning ritual; eat breakfast, talk about God, go for a boat ride, then visit Paulo, praying for news about a heart. Anna's tension kept ratcheting upward because of how quiet everything was. No more attempts on her life. No more feeling that she was being followed. Nothing. It was absolutely nerve-racking. When she wasn't spending her time with Lucas, she made herself at home on his laptop, devouring every scrap of information she could about Shawn de Chastelain, his missing brother, Brandon, and her ex-supervisor, Justin Michaels. And trying to devise a plan to get into de Chastelain's house.

And then it came—the phone call they'd been waiting for. Paulo was to get his new heart as soon as everything could be arranged.

Since things had been relatively quiet with no more problems, Anna decided it was probably okay for her to very carefully visit Paulo. She had something she wanted to give him and grinned at the thought of his reaction. Lucas had dropped her at the entrance to the hospital and gone to park the car. Hoping it wasn't the calm before the storm, she made her way through the maze of corridors, constantly keeping her eyes on the faces around her. Instead of riding the elevator, she decided at the last minute to take the stairs.

Entering the stairwell, she shifted the cheerful red-and-green box under her arm and started up, one step at a time, taking note of the sudden silence as the heavy metal door clanked shut behind her. The stillness echoed around her. About halfway up the second flight of stairs, the door clanked shut again. Muffled footsteps sounded behind her. Her nerves jumped, clamored for space. Silly. No reason to be jumpy.

Actually, she probably had good reason to be cautious. Better safe than sorry.

From her perch on the stairs, she looked down between the metal bars and saw a black-gloved hand gripping a black gun with a silencer on the end. She heard the steps coming closer, ever closer. Heart rate tripling, she realized she wasn't being jumpy or silly, she was being threatened. Dropping the package, she raced up the stairs.

Find a floor. Get to a floor. Call the cops. Oh, Lord, protect me. Don't let anyone else come into the stairwell at the wrong time.

Visions of that gun swam in her mind. Her fear of being shot nearly sent her to the floor; instead, she double-timed her pace, taking the steps two at a time. The person behind her did, too. A low laugh rumbled up toward her.

With shock, she realized he was enjoying this. He got a kick out of making her tremble with terror, making her wonder if she would get away. A chill spiked up her spine. He wasn't afraid of being caught.

Which made him extra dangerous. Not just to her, but to all the innocents in the hospital. Her muscles ached from the sudden exertion climbing the stairs two at a time required, but she ignored their protests and kept climbing, her blood humming, her heart pounding.

She passed the second-floor door, then came to the third-floor door. Paulo's floor. No way was she stopping here. The door opened and a nurse started to step into the stairwell but screeched to a halt when she saw Anna.

Without hesitating, Anna shoved the woman back onto the floor and blurted, "Call security. There's a man with a gun behind me." Not waiting for a reaction from the suddenly wide-eyed nurse, Anna aimed for the next floor, praying the woman would do as instructed.

Steps echoed. Hers? His? He was definitely closer. Her teeth clenched; panting breaths escaped. Weakness wanted to flood her, but she refused to let it. Up another floor. If she got off here, would she endanger anyone else on the floor?

Did she dare *not* get out of the stairwell?

And what if someone entered at the wrong moment, like the poor nurse had almost done? What if she'd opened the door after Anna had passed, the lunatic right behind her?

He would have shot the woman. Cold certainty made her ill.

This guy was insane for taking such a chance just to get at her.

A quick glance down allowed her to see a flash of denim, and black shoes. Then her pursuer tripped, cursed, got back on his feet. Shaking, stumbling, Anna hurried on to the next floor, determined to find a way to alert security. Seconds later, she was at the door— and stumbled to a stop. The sign in big red letters glared at her. Employees Only. The dead bolt mocked her.

No, no, no. She'd come one floor too far. Footsteps continued to thunder below her. Desperate, she hurled herself at the door and pressed against the metal bar. Nothing. Locked.

Think, think.

The climbing, unhurried footsteps echoed below her; it was only a matter of time. Then the steps stopped. A low voice hissed from the steps below, "There's no way out now. I told you to leave. You didn't listen. Now my boss wants you gone."

Terror shuddered through her. His boss?

De Chastelain.

What to do? Frantic, she darted her eyes around.

No way up.

Only down.

Past the man whose boss wanted her "gone."

Her eyes landed on the box hanging on the wall, and an idea sparked. The glass door stood open a fraction. She wouldn't even have to break in. Would it work?

Moving back into the little alcove set away from the locked door that led to safety, she reached out and pulled the heavy fire extinguisher from the wall. Could she heft it high enough to throw it? Grunting, she got a better grip, then waited.

His steps slowed, his arrogant confidence in capturing his prey evident in each calculated footfall. Then he appeared around the corner, ski-masked face revealing an evil grin. Anna swung with all her might, catching him on the shoulder. She'd been aiming for his head, but the extinguisher was too heavy for her.

His scream of pain and the sound of his falling down the stairs shot satisfaction through her. Now the tricky part. Getting past him. Not giving him time to recover, she hurtled past him, feeling his hand nearly snag her pants, then ran down to the next door, flinging it open and bursting onto the floor. Startled glances swung her way. Not caring that she looked like a crazy person, she ran to the nurses' station and said, "There's a man with a gun in the stairwell. Call 911."

Hospital policy had gone into effect immediately,

calling for emergency procedures to be implemented. Officers now swarmed the hospital. One focused on Anna, and she shivered and shook as she gave her report.

"Are you sure you saw a gun?"

She gritted her teeth, glaring at the young officer, who was beginning to get on her last nerve. "I'm sure. I know what a gun looks like."

"What about what he looked like?"

"He had on a mask, which I'm sure he pulled off as soon as I got away from him so he could walk through the hospital."

Three hours later, the officer in charge of the search and the head of hospital security approached Anna. "Ma'am, we're going to call off the search. We didn't find anyone or anything. My guess is he slipped onto one of the floors as soon as you got away from him, probably acted like he was visiting someone, then got out before we could get the hospital completely locked down. We'll check the security cameras, but don't hold your breath."

She slumped against the wall. Great. The man had gotten away, so he could strike again. As soon as the floor opened back up and the lockdown was lifted, Lucas burst through the door, the relief on his face nearly tangible as he strode over to her to catch her in a hug. Stunned, she let him. He pushed her back, hands on her biceps, worried eyes boring into hers. "Are you okay? They wouldn't let me up here until just now. When you didn't show up in Paulo's room and then the lockdown happened, I was afraid."

"De Chastelain had gotten to me?" At his nod, she

muttered, "No, but he sure got too close." Thoughtfully, she said, "It's always the hospital. Why here?"

"What do you mean?"

"He comes after me here in the hospital. Why?"

Lucas didn't speak for a moment. "Because he doesn't have access to you anywhere else. Other than trying to run us off the road, I mean. Think about it. You're pretty much at my father's house or here. Here is certainly easier to get access to you than at my father's house."

"The only time he's struck away from the hospital is when we were on the way to your home. And we were on the way home from the hospital that time. Somehow he knows when I'm here."

"And he doesn't have too many concerns about being caught."

Anna shivered. "I don't want to talk about it anymore. I want to give Paulo his gift."

"And I want to talk to Mark about some last-minute surgery preparations. Catch up to you in a little while." He pulled her close, and sighed against her head, causing shivers to run up her spine. "Stay out of trouble, please."

She gave him a light slug in the gut. "I highly doubt he'll try something else today. But thanks." Looking up, she said, "I guess once I leave today, I don't need to be coming back here, do I?"

"Probably not. But we can worry about that later tonight. See you in a bit."

Thirty minutes later, shattered nerves finally under control, Anna had retrieved her package from where she'd dropped it in the stairwell and made her way to Paulo's room.

When she crossed to the bed, he looked up, his eyes were wizened, old beyond his time, yet held a determined spark that wouldn't let go. He breathed deep, sucking in the life-giving oxygen that allowed his heart not to work so hard. His brown eyes smiled at her. "Hi, Miss Anna."

"Hi there, little guy. I brought you something."

His eyes brightened as they focused on the multicolored box still held under her arm. "What is it?"

Anna set the box on the rolling tray that held Paulo's water cup and opened the top. Reaching in, she pulled out a small, fully decorated Christmas tree.

Paulo gasped. "Oh, Miss Anna, it's beautiful."

"And it all yours. I brought it to remind you that soon you'll get to come help decorate the big one at the orphanage."

"Thank you, I love it." His eyes still wide with awe, he said, "I've never had my own Christmas tree before."

Heart clenching at the sheer joy in his voice, she cleared her throat, desperate to talk about something else so she wouldn't cry. "I hear today's the day you get your new heart."

"Yes. It is a good day, no?"

His eyes lost some of their sparkle. Anna pushed the tree to the side and leaned in to stroke his cheek. "What is it, Paulo? What's troubling you?"

Looking back up, he rested his head against the pillow and asked, "Where did my new heart come from, Miss Anna?"

She swallowed hard. How did she explain? *Lord, help. What do I say?*

"Well," she said, sitting on the bed next to him, "in order for you get a new heart, someone else has to…give it to you."

"Yes, I know this. But how is this possible? How can someone give me the heart without…"

She understood the question, she just didn't want to answer it. But she had to. "I know what you're asking, and yes, it's true, someone had to die in order for you to get a new heart."

Tears filled his eyes, lower lip trembling, and he swallowed hard. "Then I don't know if I want it. I don't want someone else to have to die so I can live."

Anna moved in to wrap his frail body in the gentlest of hugs. "I know you would never wish harm on another soul, Paulo, but the little girl that died would be happy knowing she helped someone else live. We don't want to take that away from her family, do we? I think it would be very selfish to refuse this gift she's offered."

A frown creased his forehead as he thought about that, then a huge smile crossed his face. "It is like Jesus, no? The story you told us in Bible class. He died so we can live. He offers us His free gift. If we say no, we are very selfish to make so little of His gift, yes?"

Gulping, Anna turned to see Lucas standing in the doorway. He was simply staring at Paulo. Anna would give anything to know what was going through his mind right now. She focused back on Paulo. "Yes, I couldn't agree more." The words came out husky, fighting to get around the tightness in her throat caused by damming up the tears.

Little Paulo frowned again, his thoughts already skipping ahead. "Her family must be very sad."

"Yes, they are, but knowing she's helping you makes it a little better, you know?"

He nodded. "What about Andy? When is he going to get his heart?"

"We just don't know. It's all about timing, Paulo."

A light came on behind his eyes. "I could give him my heart. From the little girl. That way Andy would be able to go home for Christmas. He talks about wanting to play on his Xbox thing. If I gave him that heart, he could do that, yes?" He folded his little arms across his chest and gave a short nod. "Yes, that is what we must do. You must give the heart to Andy. That way the gift will not be wasted and I will wait for the next one."

Anna didn't know whether to laugh or cry. This beautiful, unselfish child who had nothing was willing to give up…everything…for his friend. She couldn't speak, just stared helplessly at Lucas, who finally found his own voice to explain. "Sorry, bud. It doesn't quite work that way. You're very generous to want to help Andy, but the blood type has to match. This heart from the little girl is just about as perfect a match as we can get for you. If we put it in Andy's body, his body wouldn't like it and that would just make Andy even more sick. No, this one is special just for you."

Paulo's lips puckered in thought again, his little brows pulling downward. "Oh. Then I must accept this gift. We must not waste it. It is the right thing to do."

Lucas gripped Paulo's bony shoulder. "I'm glad you see it that way."

The boy slid down further in the bed and closed his eyes. "I'm very tired now. I think I will sleep some before I get the new heart."

Anna and Lucas left him, stepping into the hallway. As soon as the door shut behind her, she burst into tears. Lucas didn't say a word, just pulled her into his arms and let her get it out. Finally, she looked up and gave self-conscious half laugh through the tears. "I'm sorry.

I'm a mess. I just can't believe that child in there. He's so unspoiled, so innocent and unselfish. I think we could all learn a few things from him."

Lucas pressed a gentle kiss to her forehead before pulling her back into a hug. "I couldn't agree more." He whispered the words so softly, she almost didn't catch them, but she did and realized God was doing something in this man's heart. Joy bubbled inside her at the idea of Lucas becoming a Christian. *Please, Lord, keep working on him. Keep showing him Your unconditional love.*

Lucas felt blown away by Paulo's willingness to sacrifice himself so that another boy could live. He wondered if Paulo was even aware that this was his one shot at life. That he was very close to death and if this operation didn't take place or work for some reason, he probably wouldn't live to see very many more tomorrows.

And then he decided, yes, the boy knew.

What was inside him that made him so unselfish, so willing to make that kind of sacrifice? The kid was only nine years old. Where had he seen that kind of giving?

His eyes slid to the woman seated by his side. Anna.

She'd taught Paulo about God. About a God that offered himself up as a sacrifice so that others could live. And she'd taught him that, as a follower of Christ, he was to strive to be like Jesus. Paulo wanted to be like the Jesus he loved, which was what made him willingly to give away the one thing that would allow him to live here on this earth.

Lucas shook his head. It was beginning to throb with all this thinking about God. And yet, it seemed he couldn't *stop* thinking about Him. Maybe it was time to give God a chance. What could it hurt? He pressed the button on the elevator, still deep in thought.

He headed for his meeting with Mark relieved to switch his thoughts from spiritual things. Paulo was being prepped now. Anna would stay with him until the surgery. Lucas had explained everything to Paulo in as much detail as possible about what to expect pre-op and post-op.

Paulo didn't much like the idea of waking up with a tube down his throat, nor the fact that he would be unable to speak. But Lucas promised him in a few weeks he would be feeling so much better it would all be worth it in the end.

After the routine meeting, Lucas headed to find Paulo. He'd promised to be in the surgery with him. The boy had specifically asked him to be there and Lucas had agreed. He would hold his hand until the anesthesia kicked in. Then he would watch…and maybe pray. Just to see.

He met them coming down the hall toward the operating room. Paulo sighed in relief when he saw Lucas. "I knew you would come. You said you would."

Lucas grabbed Paulo's hand. "Hey, you're my bud. No way would I let you down."

They walked hand in hand, Anna trotting on the other side of the gurney to the surgery center. Stopping outside the door, Anna leaned over to press a kiss to Paulo's cheek. "I'll be waiting on you when you come out, okay? Remember that Jesus is there with you, holding you tight."

"Yes. I am not worried."

The gurney started forward and Anna stepped back.

"Wait," Paulo said. The gurney stopped. He looked at Lucas and Anna and said, "I want to pray. Is it okay?"

Uncomfortable, Lucas shuffled his feet a little. Anna jumped right in. "Of course it's okay. Do you want to or do you want me to?"

"You prayed in the room. Now I will say the prayer on my heart. My old heart."

He still held on to Lucas's hand and reached again for Anna's. She took it, bowing her head. Lucas cleared his throat but didn't argue.

"Dear Jesus, this is Paulo. I thank You for the gift of this new heart. I know the girl's family is sad and missing her. Please tell them that she is okay and that she is with You, so she is very happy right now. Thank You for sending Miss Anna to watch over me since my own mama is also with You. Miss Anna is a very good mama so that I don't miss mine so much now. Thank You for Ella, too. I am a lucky boy because it's like I almost have two mamas." He paused to draw in a shuddering breath.

Lucas didn't know how much longer Anna was going to be able to hold it together, but she was giving it her best effort. He almost motioned for the tech to start the journey into the surgery room, but Paulo wasn't finished yet.

"And I pray for my doctor Lucas. He is very sad sometimes, but he is a very good doctor. I don't think he has Your gift, though, so could You please give him a new heart, too? But one that has You in it. I think he would be much happier then. And please send my friend Andy a new heart, too. That's all, God. Please give the doctors a good day. Amen."

Lucas coughed, felt tears push behind his eyes. They

had to get that boy in surgery or he and Anna both would be one big sobbing, slobbering mess. He almost thanked God himself when the gurney finally disappeared behind the double doors. When he turned to Anna, silent tears tracked their way down her cheeks and he gave in to the urge to pull her to him. She rested her forehead on his chest, and her arms encircled his waist to link her hands at the small of his back. He whispered, "He'll be fine."

"Sure, I know that."

"He prayed for me."

She nodded against his chest. "I noticed that, too."

"He didn't say a word about himself."

"No, he wouldn't."

Lucas swallowed hard. "I'm going to go be with him."

"Yeah, you do that. I'm going to go pray."

"Yeah…me, too." *Okay, God, I think You've got me. I also think I'm at the point where I might need to start praying and let You take control. We'll talk about this later, okay?*

EIGHT

It was morning, her tenth day back in the United States and she basked in what had quickly become her favorite time of the day. The boathouse stood quiet as the sun first peeked over the horizon, then came on up to get a full look at the new day. Fortunately, there'd been no more evidence of the man who attacked her in the stairwell at the hospital. That relieved—and bothered—her.

As she waited for Lucas, Anna pushed the disturbing memories away, prayed, thanked God for the blessings He'd bestowed lately. Paulo was out of surgery and everything had gone smoothly.

Anna had been there when Paulo had first awakened from the surgery. Unfortunately, the little guy had been in a good deal of pain, crying until the nurse upped his pain meds. Once the drugs kicked in, he'd relaxed and fallen back into a deep sleep. He'd be in the intensive-care unit for about a week, then would have another three to four weeks in the hospital. Then he could go home. Of course he would be on the autoimmune system drugs for the rest of his life, but at least he would have a "rest of his life."

Ella would stay with Paulo around the clock since it

would be impossible for Anna to care for him like he needed. Unfortunately, she had no idea if she would have to disappear with no notice or not. And she certainly didn't want to put Paulo in any danger if de Chastelain and his crew decided to come after her again. Which she fully expected to happen, and because she expected it, her nerves stayed stretched tight—waiting.

Things had been awfully quiet. However, with no news from Justin, and Shawn de Chastelain's incessant gloating, via his spokesperson, on national TV about being released from prison soon, Anna felt goaded into action. Somehow, she had to find a way into that house.

With the weird tingling in the pit of her stomach and an aching longing in her heart, Anna watched Lucas make his way toward her wearing a navy-blue fisherman's sweater with a matching knit cap pulled over his ears. Frost greeted each breath he took, mimicking the steam from the twin cups of steaming coffee he held, one in each hand. Blue jeans rode snug on his lean frame and the hiking boots assured him of a steady step.

Anna had on a new heavy coat, zipped to her chin. Later, the morning would warm up and she would most likely discard it to the bottom of the boat.

"Ready?"

"For coffee, sure." She took the proffered cup and sipped, letting the warmth of the steam wash over her frozen nose.

"Very funny. Ready to ride?"

"Yep. I think it's getting colder each morning, though."

"Definitely. Christmas will be here before we know it."

"Do you think we could make time for some shopping? I need to get a few things."

"What are you doing for Thanksgiving, Anna? It's only a couple of weeks away."

"No plans as of today, why?"

"What about your family? Friends? You must have somebody somewhere."

She shrugged. "Nope. After my grandmother died, I spent two years of my life in foster homes and was on my own from the age of eighteen. I told you that."

A frown creased his forehead. "I know. I guess it's just hard for me to fathom that you have no one."

"Sounds pretty pitiful when you put it that way." She headed down to the boat. "After my parents were killed in a car accident when I was twelve, my grandmother took me in. And all I can say is the woman was incredible." The wind off the water whipped her dark curls around her face. She brushed them back thinking she'd soon need a haircut. "Anyway, she got me through the beginning of the horrid teen years. A year before she died, I accepted Christ. He's been my rock ever since. As for friends, we've lost touch. At first because of my job, then later I was in Brazil, of course." She shrugged. "Making friends here could get them killed. It didn't seem worth it."

Lucas trailed a finger down her cheek, the longing in his eyes causing an oxygen shortage in her lungs. She pulled back and he gave a resigned smile, but didn't address her skittishness. He climbed on board the luxury craft. The first time she'd seen it, she'd dubbed it the floating house. He turned and held up a hand to help her aboard. She placed her hand in his, relishing the feel of his rough calluses against the smoothness of her palm.

He said, "Well, I know one friend you've got."

Anna shivered at the gentle sweetness and resisted

the urge to lean in closer to him. She'd just backed away a minute ago, no sense in sending conflicting signals.

Safely on board, he gave her hand a last squeeze then headed to start the boat, leaving her wishing for more.

The engine rumbled quietly, a mere vibration under her feet, as Lucas steered the craft out into the cove away from the pier. Anna stood on deck shivering with delight as the cool morning air rushed over her. Goose bumps pimpled her flesh, but she didn't mind. Sharing this time with Lucas had become a special treat.

Waves slapped the sides of the craft as she watched Lucas drive. He grinned at her, his face alive, two deep dimples peeking out from his clean-shaven cheeks to send shivers spinning through her stomach. Oh my, she was so attracted to him. And yet, his eyes never seemed to have peace. They remained haunted even when he gave the appearance of being happy. *God, he's so special. I didn't realize just how much I really wanted to be with him until recently. But I know he doesn't belong to You yet, so keep working on him. I think he's really close, especially after Paulo's prayer.*

The *thump, thump, thump* of a helicopter caught her attention and she gazed up at it, thinking it seemed to be flying awfully low. The wind stirred, becoming harsher, rocking the boat, whipping her dark curls in a disorganized dance. Glancing at Lucas's face through the window, she could see he was perturbed. He motioned for her to join him inside behind the protection of the glass. As she stood, she saw the glint of something in the doorway of the chopper. Then what looked like a barrel of a...

Gun!

With that thought, bullets splattered the helm of the craft. Anna screamed for Lucas as she ran for the door that would take her belowdecks and hopefully offer some kind of buffer from the spray of bullets.

Thwap, thwap.

Before she could reach the door, Lucas appeared in front of her, something in his hand. With his free hand, he grabbed her, pulling her into the protection of the boat. With his other, he pointed at the helicopter. It was only then she realized he had a flare gun. Ducking against another spray of bullets, she pulled him down with her, her FBI training kicking in. Forcing aside the terror flowing through her at the thought of being shot again, she focused on surviving…and keeping Lucas alive.

"Stay down, you're going to get killed! Give me the gun! I have a better shot from this angle." Something in her tone must have registered and he pushed it into her outstretched hand. Peering around the glass, she watched the helicopter drop lower. She aimed, waited, just a little lower, then pulled the trigger. Her aim was off by a margin but still, the flare hit the tail of the chopper, knocking it sideways. It spun in the air, the pilot grappling for control. He managed to pull it up slightly, then physics won and the helicopter spun toward the ocean…and the boat. She saw two bodies bail out at the last moment. Who were they? From the corner of her eye, she noticed a speedboat racing across the waves.

Lucas grabbed her hand and yelled, "Jump!"

And over the side they went.

Water closed in over her, the frigid cold stealing what little breath she'd managed to gasp just before she went under. Lucas still had her hand in a death grip. She struggled, needed to swim up, needed another breath of air, but he kicked, pulled her behind him. Understanding his silent signal, instead of fighting him, she kicked, helping, doing her best to get away from the attackers; ignoring her desperate need for oxygen.

She let out a few air bubbles to see which way was up.

Jerking on his hand, she got his attention and pointed to the surface. He frowned, shook his head.

She had to have air or she would pass out, which would do neither of them any good at all.

He must have seen something frantic in her expression as he relented and kicked, propelling them upward. Finally, they broke the surface, and Anna gasped in much needed air.

She looked back at the boat.

And watched the helicopter slam into it.

The two crafts burst into flames, the explosion rocking the ocean and sending waves over their heads. Still they swam, frantic to get away from the burning ball of fire and the pull of the water as the metal screeched and groaned, slowly sinking below the surface.

Pulling it loose, she shrugged out of her heavy coat, watching as the next wave carried it away. She kicked out of her shoes and that's when the cold hit her. Shivering, teeth chattering, she shuddered, barely able to force her arms to work. "I'm f-f-freezing. We have t-t-to get to shore."

"Swim," he ordered. Anna noticed his lips turning blue. She also noticed he'd managed to unlace and kick off his heavy hiking boots. Swimming was the last thing she wanted to do, but she forced herself to head to the dock that looked absolutely minuscule in the distance. Thank God they hadn't gone that far out. At least they could still see land.

Lucas heard her suck in a deep breath and whisper his name. Terror and cold siphoned the energy from her and she went under. He followed, grasped her arm and pulled her, gasping, back up. "Come on, Miss FBI agent, pull yourself together."

He goaded her, hiding his own fear. It was cold and they had a long way to swim.

Anna's grip on his right hand had already cut the circulation off. He pulled her closer, kicking his feet to stay afloat; he was wasting his energy staying in one spot. "Come on, head for shore."

"Right," she chattered, panting, blowing breaths to keep her calm. "Right, I'm already exhausted and I'm supposed to swim. Sure. Okay. Let's go."

He shook his head at this amazing woman. Scared spitless, she still managed to surprise him. Visibly, she gathered her wits.

Slowly, they made their way toward the beach, keeping a watchful eye on the water surrounding them. The cold made for sluggish swimming. Lucas mustered his strength, but real fear caught him in the middle as he realized how tired he was growing and they still had about half a mile to go before reaching shore.

He stopped, let his face dip below the water as he held his breath. His heavy clothing pulled him down. Anna's was doing the same to her. When he came back up, her terror grabbed him. "Lucas, we're not going to make it." Her breaths came in short puffs, and the wind whipped around them. Cold had turned his hands into useless slabs of flesh. His legs felt leaden.

This time Anna went under then fought her way back up. Lucas tried to help by pulling her but wasn't sure if he managed to help or hinder.

A noise caught his attention. At first he thought it was another helicopter coming back to make another pass and unleash another volley of bullets, but then he saw the speck on the water growing closer.

Anna floated on her back, eyes closed, lips moving. He knew she was praying.

He joined her as he watched the motorboat. Worry ate at him. Was it whoever had been in the helicopter? Coming back to finish the job? Lucas knew if it was, there was no way they'd survive; no way to outswim the boat.

Please, get us out of this, God. At least get Anna out. She doesn't deserve this.

Anna continued to float, arms splayed, lips still moving. Lucas moved in closer, a strange peace invading his entire chilled being. How much longer could they stay in the water until hypothermia set in?

The boat made its way closer and Lucas breathed a sigh of pure relief—and thankfulness. He recognized it as one of his father's crafts. "Ted."

Anna stirred, sluggishly opening her eyes; she saw the boat and tears leaked down her cheeks. Now that they were so very close to safe, she could break down. He felt like joining her.

"Ted, get her in the boat. We're freezing!"

Ted's eyes, wide with the shock of what he'd just witnessed, hurried to fling the ladder over the side. Lucas ignored his own uncontrollable shuddering and pulled Anna toward the ladder.

* * *

Anna gripped the ladder's rail and placed feet with no feeling on the first rung. Numbness pervaded her, but the instinct to survive pushed her; the hands gripping her forearms pulled. And she was in the boat.

Ted grabbed Lucas. Anna added her own feeble strength and, somehow, they managed to haul him over the side. He lay on the floor of the craft, shaking so hard he appeared to be convulsing. Anna threw herself down beside him, grabbed him around the shoulders and cried. His arm came up around her shoulder for a reassuring pat.

Ted gunned the motor and head for the pier.

Anna hollered over the roar, "Did you bring a cell phone?"

Ted nodded, "I already called 911. They should be waiting on us when we get there."

Upon their arrival at the pier, the next few hours passed in a fuzzy blur for Anna. She was loaded into an ambulance, checked out, poked and prodded, transferred to a medical helicopter, airlifted to the hospital where she was unloaded and the whole poking and prodding process started all over again.

As she was wheeled from the helicopter, grogginess grabbed at her. Then the medicine kicked in and darkness closed over her.

NINE

Two days later, Lucas woke to see his father peering down at him. "So, you cheated death again."

Lucas groaned. Did he have to deal with this now? He'd just given his statement to the police and didn't feel like adding any more stress to his day. He closed his eyes then peeked. The man stayed put. Okay, he was going to have to deal with him.

"Hello, Father. The survival instinct is strong—and I think God was…merciful and knew I wasn't ready to face Him just yet."

"Ah, so you got religion out there?"

Lucas flinched, the same sarcastic words he spoken to his father only a few days ago returning to haunt him. Instead of firing back, he paused then said slowly, "I believe there's a God out there, and I'm taking the time to talk to him a little."

Surprise flickered on the older man's features. He seemed to be at a loss for words. Lucas chuckled to himself. Well, well, would wonders never cease?

His father reached out, touched his hand briefly before pulling back. Gruffly, almost grudgingly, he said, "Thought I was going to lose you. That I was going to have to go through another one of those awful periods of waiting to identify your body—or at least wait an eternity for another DNA match. Thanks for having the decency to spare me that." After the explosion, the only thing forensics had found of his brother's body had been a tooth. They'd had to live through the agonizing ordeal of waiting for what they already knew…the DNA matched that of Lance Bennett.

Shocked, Lucas could only stare up at this man he called Father. Never could he remember the man being so open about his feelings. The stoic look was gone, and a rare vulnerability shone through so briefly he wondered if he'd imagined it.

The door to his room opened. Thomas's expression went blank, returning to his usual stern countenance, but Lucas smiled as he welcomed his cousin. "Godfrey, you didn't have to come all the way out here. How are you?"

Godfrey looked angry, worried. "I think that should be my line, don't you?"

Lucas shrugged. "I've been better, but at least I'm alive to talk about it."

"Leave it to you to bring excitement back into our lives."

"Excitement I can do without." His features hardened. "Did they catch the guys in that chopper? Anna saw them bail out at the last minute and some kind of speedboat picked them up. I'm sure if the guys in the helicopter had failed, the guys in the boat were supposed to finish the job. I'm also sure the helicopter crashing sent them all running. They knew someone would be there pretty fast."

His cousin shook his head. "They got away. Ted saw

the whole thing. He called it in and gave as much detail to the cops as he could. Anna gave her statement this morning. The police will try to salvage what they can of the helicopter, but it's in pieces at the bottom of the ocean."

Anxiety flitted across his chest. He wanted to see her, her smile, touch her cheek. "How is she? They told me she was all right and recovering from some hypothermia, but should be back to normal soon with some rest."

"Same thing they told you about your own stubborn self, if I remember correctly." Mark Priestly had his head stuck around the door. He gave a furtive glance behind him then turned to Lucas. "You've got a visitor."

Anna, Lucas thought, his heart accelerating, eager to see her.

His surprise was genuine when Mark stepped aside to allow the woman his brother had planned to marry to sweep through the door. He gaped. "Marybeth Ferris? What are you doing here?"

She pulled to a quick halt, staring at him. Lucas cocked his head to the left studying her, wondering why she was here, what she was up to now. A French-manicured hand covered her lips. One perfectly arched eyebrow nearly started a new part at her hairline. "I…I'm sorry. It's just—" she swallowed hard "—you look…seeing you…"

Taking pity on the shell-shocked woman, Lucas quirked a half smile and said, "It's okay, Marybeth, I know it's got to be unsettling to see me. I think the last time we saw each other was Lance's funeral, right?"

She nodded, gathered her composure, greeted Godfrey then shot a glance at Thomas Bennett. The man cleared his throat. "Good to see you, Marybeth."

"And you, sir." Her eyes never left Lucas even though she spoke to his father. Fully recovered from her initial shock of seeing Lucas and absorbing that although he looked exactly like the man she'd once loved, he was an entirely different person, she gave a sultry half smile, resting a hand on Lucas's forearm. "I've been waiting a long time for you to come home, Lucas."

Dread crept up Lucas's stomach. Uh-oh, Marybeth's presence wasn't unplanned, of that he was sure. But surely it hadn't been his father who... He watched as his father stepped to Marybeth's side and slid an arm around her shoulders. Lucas felt the searing heat of that blue gaze singe him as his father unblinking, unbelievably, said, "Lucas, I asked Marybeth to come. I've told her that you two would have my blessing if you decided to get married and provide me with a grandson."

Anna stopped, her hand on the door to Lucas's room. Shock, not to mention hurt and anger, rippled through her as she caught Lucas's father's last few words. Lucas and another woman? He'd never mentioned anything of the sort and she'd never even entertained the idea that he might have someone here. She was puzzled. Was he that good an actor? She never would have guessed he'd been toying with her, building a relationship only to have it mean nothing to him because of the woman in this room.

Hand still resting on the door, she debated her options. Did she want to go in there and face the fact that Lucas could very well belong to someone else? Not that he belonged to *her,* of course, but if she walked in that room, she could find out there never would be anything between them. And yet…she should probably give Lucas the benefit of the doubt, let him tell her what was going on. She pushed open the door and slipped inside. Inside the room, she saw Lucas still hooked up to an IV, a tall blond standing beside him, her hand resting comfortably on his arm. A rush of sickness curled in her stomach. Looking into Lucas's eyes, she silently questioned him with raised eyebrows. Lucas, looking extremely uncomfortable and very glad to see her, cleared his throat. "Marybeth, I'd like you to meet Anna Freeman. Anna, this is Marybeth Ferris. She was Lance's fiancée before he died."

A smidgen of relief spread through her as she nodded to the woman, yet still, she knew what she'd heard standing outside the door. Thomas Bennett approved of a relationship between this woman and Lucas. From his reaction the other morning at breakfast, he obviously didn't consider Anna's blood blue enough. That hurt, but she brushed it off.

Godfrey spoke. "Hello, Anna. Glad to see you're none the worse for wear after your little swim."

"Thank you, Godfrey. It was a lot more excitement than I'd bargained for, but I'm very thankful everything turned out all right. The police came by my room and I gave them a statement, so I guess there's nothing left to do but wait and see what they come up with."

Godfrey said, "They're working on pulling up the pieces left of the boat and the helicopter. But I wouldn't hold out much hope for any evidence. Both were pretty much destroyed. At least that's what one of the officers said."

Eyes narrowed, Lucas said, "You can bet I'm going to do all I can to find out who's trying to get you, Anna."

At this statement, warmth and fear slid through her veins. There was no way she was going to let Lucas, an excellent doctor but with no skills in dealing with criminals and the like, try to track down a killer. That was her job. She had the training. She just had to get over the fear that crowded her throat every time she thought about doing it. Unconsciously, her hand moved to her abdomen.

Lucas noticed and asked, "Are you sure you're all right?"

She jerked her hand away, smoothed it down her jeans and forced a smile. "Sure. I just need to figure out what to do. Who to call for help." She really didn't want to call Justin until she had figured out if he was the one who had betrayed her by letting de Chastelain know she was back in town. But she needed help from someone, as she was—once again—in over her head.

Thirty minutes later, Lucas was unhooked from all of his wires and they'd been discharged faster than Anna had ever experienced with a hospital. No doubt thanks to Lucas's father. Or maybe it was because Lucas was a doctor himself. He knew how to work the system.

Ted was waiting to take everyone home, but Lucas said, "I want to stay at the hospital and visit Paulo." Shooting a questioning look at Thomas, Lucas asked, "Could I get a car delivered?"

Surprisingly enough, Thomas graciously agreed after repeated assurances that Lucas felt up to driving. Godfrey had driven his own car and offered to walk Marybeth down to hers. She pouted about it, clung to Lucas's arm and beseeched him with her eyes.

He ignored her and Anna hated the sweet relief that flowed through her. She shouldn't feel so territorial about a man who would most likely never be hers. The ping of grief that pierced her nearly made her gasp. Refusing to study it, Anna instead tried to figure out what had gone wrong, and who she could call for help. And decide whether to confront Justin now or wait until she felt better.

Desperate to get away from the hospital before anything else happened, Anna decided to think it all out on the way home. After a brief visit with Paulo they headed down to the parking garage. Lucas called and asked his father where to find the car. Godfrey had volunteered to ride in and help Ted deliver it as he had a dinner meeting and would just have Ted drive him home when he was finished. The car sat like a sleek cougar waiting to unleash restrained power.

Laughing, Anna teased, "The VIP lot. Must be nice to be such an important guy."

Lucas flipped his phone closed and stuck it in his back pocket. He slanted her a glance and a mock scowl. "That's my father's doing, not mine, I assure you."

"I know, Lucas, you don't have to defend yourself to me."

They climbed into the car. Lucas buckled his seat belt but didn't start the engine. "You're thinking about leaving again, aren't you?"

Mentally, she groaned. How did he do that? "Lucas, I've put you in danger several times now. Even though we've hired a guard to watch his room now, I don't think I can come back to the hospital anymore, either. Not even to see Paulo. I've been attacked here twice and felt threatened once."

"I understand. I think that's probably a wise decision."

"You do?"

"Yeah. Paulo's okay. Ella's with him. It's you we need to focus on."

"There can be no 'we' right now, Lucas. I need you to leave me alone and let me do my job. Worrying about you is just adding to my stress."

Lucas looked away for a moment. "Who do you trust, Anna?"

"What?"

"Who do you trust? Do you trust Justin?"

Chewing her lip, she studied the sky outside. It looked like it was going to rain. Great. She sighed. Did she trust Justin? *Could* she trust him? He was the only one who knew where she was. The absolute only person she'd been in contact with who had anything to do with her past. Of course, she'd been in the FBI office and someone could have possibly recognized her, but it wasn't likely. Plus the threats had started before then. She finally said, "I don't know. I've talked to him for four years and I've never had a problem. Then again, I never told him where I was, either, taking extra pains to keep my location untraceable. I didn't tell him where I was in the beginning simply because it seemed…safer that way and I just continued that pattern over the years. And I knew as soon as I used my passport, he'd know about it."

Blowing out a breath, she said, "I just don't get the vibe that he wants me dead. What I'm thinking is that maybe he trusted the wrong person. It could be that he told someone in the department I was back and either *that* someone is a traitor or that someone told another someone." She glanced up at Lucas. "You get the idea."

"I suppose that's possible."

"I just can't imagine that de Chastelain would have someone staked out to watch the airport for the past four years just waiting for me to come home. I mean, I could have flown into any other state then taken a bus or a train. Of course, if he had a line on my passport like Justin…"

"True." Lucas started the car, ready to get the drive back to North Carolina over with. "So, what are you going to do? Are you going to call Justin or not?"

"I suppose I owe him the chance to explain—if he can."

"You don't owe him anything if he's trying to kill you."

"But what if it's not him? Sure, all the evidence points toward him right now, but what if it's all circumstantial? What if I blame him, don't turn to him for help and it's not him?" She rubbed her aching eyes. "I'm tired. I need to go back to your house, pack, and find a place to stay. I can't put you or your family in any more danger."

"I really wish you'd reconsider. That house has a superior security system. The neighborhood is gated. You're much safer there than going out on your own. We're all safe there. I'll even hire extra security if it'll make you feel better."

"Lucas! They got us out on the ocean, remember? They can approach the house from the water. No. I just can't."

Jaw clenched, lips tight, he didn't say anything more. Instead, he put the car in gear and pulled out of the parking lot, heading for Standing Wave Highway toward North Carolina.

How could he convince her to stay? What would it take for her to realize she had to have some kind of help? And not necessarily Justin's. If the man wasn't the one who'd betrayed her, then he'd said something to someone who couldn't be trusted. And if that was the case, she was truly on her own, unable to turn to the organization she'd once worked for.

And there was no way he was going to allow her to bear this burden alone. He'd be there for her, see her through this. Convincing her to let him was going to be an exercise in stubbornness on his part. He thought out his strategy, trying to come up with an argument she couldn't refute.

While he thought, he drove on auto pilot, heading down the hill that would lead them home. He pressed the brake, then scooted around the slower moving car in front of him. "I meant what I said, Anna. I'm in this with you to the end. You're going to have to have help, someone you can trust."

"I never said I didn't trust Justin."

"No, you didn't *say* that."

She glanced at him from the corner of her eye then let out a disgusted huff. "Stop reading my mind, Bennett."

"It's not mind reading, it's simply knowing how you think." Which was scary for him as he'd never had that kind of…connection with a woman before. Oh, he'd dated, even had one serious relationship with a woman his father had deemed suitable for him to marry. But he'd come to his senses before his one out-of-character attempt to please his father had completely wrecked his life. Then Lance had died…

"Lucas, you're going kind of fast, you want to slow down?"

Lucas snapped back to the road, his attention momentarily distracted by his thoughts. "Oh, sorry."

He pressed the brake.

Nothing happened.

Frowning, he pressed harder.

This time the pedal went to the floor.

"Uh-oh."

Anna's head swiveled to look at him. "Don't say that. I hate those words. Why would you say 'uh-oh'? No, don't tell me." She held up a hand forestalling his explanation. "I don't want to know. I've had too many uh-ohs in the last forty-eight hours. No more uh-ohs okay?"

"Are you done?"

She groaned. "What is it?"

"We don't have any brakes."

TEN

Immediately, she turned serious, her face losing color. She swallowed hard. "Oh, I didn't know it was that kind of 'uh-oh'. Tell me what to do."

"Hold on tight and pray."

"I don't suppose the gas tank would be close to empty or anything, would it?"

"Nope," he yanked the steering wheel to the right, the road sloping downward, the car gaining speed.

"Emergency brake?"

"Already tried it, not working." He pumped it so as to prove his point.

"Can you throw it in Park?"

Without glancing her way, he said, "Not without scattering the transmission all over the highway and possibly losing control of the steering. I've got it in the lowest gear, but it's not doing me much good on this downhill stretch. I'm wondering if someone tampered with the car."

Scenery whipped by even faster. Fortunately, even though they were going downhill, there wasn't much traffic and he could see a good distance in front of them. The bad news was, about three miles ahead, there was a busy intersection with a traffic light. They were on a downhill stretch on an otherwise pretty flat road. Once they were through the intersection the road would switch to more of an uphill grade and the car would slow, possibly even stop, but first they had to make it though that intersection.

"Call 911 and warn them I'm going to be coming through that intersection and they need to have someone there to stop the traffic. If the light's green, great. If not…" He whipped into the next lane, around a slower-moving vehicle.

"Uh-oh."

Anna looked up from getting her phone and gasped. "Go around them."

Gritting his teeth, Lucas watched the two semis ride side by side, blocking both lanes. He couldn't go to the left because of the dividing rail. If he went to the right, he'd be right on the edge, running up onto the sidewalk and possibly into one of the stores lining the road or—worse—a pedestrian. He laid on his horn, blasting the warning he was coming up behind them.

Either they didn't hear him, or they ignored him.

With the distance closing fast, Lucas had a decision to make. Anna kept her cool on the phone with the dispatcher. And still Lucas blared the horn.

If they got out of this alive, she was leaving. Because of her, Lucas was now a target. The two trucks didn't move even though Lucas still laid on the horn. Congestion waited a short distance ahead and the road showed no signs of leveling out. Anna had relayed their desperation to the operator, and about a minute later, a highway patrol car came barreling up behind them, blue lights flashing.

Out of the corner of her eye she caught sight of a car pulling up to a side street just ahead—then inching forward. Horror gripped Anna as she realized the car was going to go for it and pull out in front of them.

"Lucas, watch out!" *Please, God, please, God, don't let them pull out.* Lucas muttered under his breath as the car zipped out into the middle of the right-hand lane. He wrenched the wheel, steering the car into the left lane, tires squealing at the sudden direction change. The digital speedometer read seventy-six. The speed limit was fifty-five.

Anna breathed a sigh of temporary relief as they flew past without a collision. The patrol car kept up, the blue lights causing other cars to take note. Just as Lucas was about to close in on the tail of one of the semis, it put on a burst of speed. The other one slowed, and Lucas slipped in between to pull in front of the slower-moving truck. Maybe the officer behind them had gotten one of the truck drivers on the radio. Anna didn't really care how it happened, she was just glad it had.

"Ma'am, are you there? Ma'am?"

Anna dimly realized she still held the phone to her ear and the 911 operator was still on the line. "I'm here. But we're almost to that intersection." Her cell phone beeped. She looked at the screen. Justin. He'd have to wait.

"There's should be a patrol car there soon. He's about a minute away."

"Yeah, well, so are we. He needs to be thirty seconds away."

"He's working on it. Can you see the light?"

"Not yet." A memory hit her. "Lucas, if you can get through this intersection, the stores and sidewalks end and it becomes open fields. You might be able to get off the highway and into one of those fields."

"Yeah, I remember." White knuckles glared at her from their grip on the steering wheel. Lucas's body shouted his intense concentration as his eyes flicked from side to side, mirror to mirror. "So pray me through this intersection."

Anna's eyes widened as she took in the crowd they were coming up on. Three patrol cars sat off the highway and out of the way. Two patrolmen held up traffic. Lucas's palm hit the horn again. The lane was clear except for one car and another patrolman who was frantically waving it out of the way. And then they were closer, closer. Lucas whipped around, barely out of the way and they shot under the red light without incident. Anna wilted against the seat.

"It's not over yet. I need an uphill grade to slow us down some before I try getting off the highway."

She picked up the phone. The operator still waited. "We're through the intersection."

The road slanted upward, and the speedometer dropped to seventy, then sixty-five, slowing on down to finally hit thirty. Cars buzzed around them. The two patrol officers caught up with them, giving them an escort to the side of the road, away from the traffic and onto the grass. They bumped and bounced a short distance until Lucas put the car straight from Drive into Reverse then Park.

And then they were still.

And Anna just sat there.

Lucas blew out a breath. Adrenaline still pumped through his blood, but he knew when it wore off he'd want to sleep for a week. Looking over at Anna, he noticed her empty stare. She hadn't moved since they'd rolled to a stop. Hadn't said a word or blinked.

"Hey." He reached over and took her ice-cold hand in his. "You okay?"

At first she didn't answer, then without looking at him—or blinking—she said, "No. I'm mad."

She didn't look mad. She looked almost catatonic.

"Okay." He pondered what to say then looked into her eyes. What he saw there made him feel almost sorry for whoever was after her. He'd seen Anna upset, afraid, angry, in the spirit of worship, joyful, hurting for a sick child, but never this—this tightly leashed rage that needed a place to explode.

Yet when she spoke, she spoke with slow, measured words, her tone frigid. "I'm really, really mad."

He cleared his throat. "Yeah, I can see that. So what do you want to do about it?"

Sucking in a deep breath, she closed her eyes then let the breath whistle from her lips in one long soft puff. When she opened them, the rage still simmered in their crystalline blue depths, but he could also see her thinking.

She said, "You know, I've been scared. Terrified to come back here."

"But?"

"I don't think I'm scared anymore." She said it thoughtfully, as though it surprised her to be able to admit that. Lucas wondered if she was in shock. Then she looked at him again and he didn't see any signs of shock, just sheer determination and bulldog stubbornness.

Finished with *yet another* police report, Lucas had dropped her at the front entrance then driven back to the garage to park *yet another* rental car out of the way until he could return it tomorrow. Unsure who to trust, Anna refused to call Justin with this latest incident. It seemed someone knew her every move and she was tired of it, tired of putting people she cared about in danger. Her mind made up, Anna fully intended to go straight to her room to pack and vacate the premises. On her way through the foyer that led to the staircase, she noticed the name on the invitation lying innocently on the side table. The envelope had been opened, the invitation in plain sight, there for anyone to read. So she read it.

You are invited to a celebration/charity auction
celebrating the homecoming of
Shawn de Chastelain
To be held at the home of
Shawn and Sherry de Chastelain
Saturday Night, November 22nd
7:00 p.m.
A buffet will be served
Come prepared to raise money for abused
children
Bids start at a minimum of $5,000
Goal: $5,000,000
RSVP

So, he was out of jail. And trying to sweep everything under the rug with a good deed. As if a charity auction would wipe away the memory of his crimes. She snorted. Of course the Bennett family would be invited. Thomas Bennett was a longstanding member of the upper class, involved in local business and charities. And Godfrey was just as influential since moving in and taking over parts of the business and starting a successful business of his own with his wife.

Her phone chirped again, indicating a missed call and she remembered Justin beeping in on her when she'd been on the phone with the 911 operator. He'd probably been calling to let her know de Chastelain had been released.

The anger she'd felt only a couple of weeks before ripped through her again, then faded to the background of her mind as a plan started formulating. She glanced at the invitation again. The party was just a little over a week away, the Saturday after Thanksgiving and Anna realized she'd just found her way into the de Chastelain home.

She'd probably need the actual invitation—or at least a good copy—to get through the gate and into the house. Glancing around to make sure she was alone, she palmed the invitation and slipped it into her back pocket. Surely, somewhere in this house, there was a printer to make a copy on.

The door slammed and she jumped, whirling to see Marybeth Ferris, Lance's fiancée, enter the foyer. The woman stopped short as though surprised to see Anna standing in the foyer. Snapping golden eyes narrowed, a slight smile lifted the corners of red-tinted lips. "Hello. Anna, right?"

"Yes." Anna offered a smile of her own. "Can I help you?"

"Do you really think you have a chance with him?"

Anna let the shutters fall over her eyes, her expression carefully neutral. She pretended ignorance. "Excuse me?"

"So that's the way you want to play it." Her top lip

curled. "Well, let me fill you in on a few facts, darling. Lucas is all his father has left. Trust me when I say the man wants grandchildren and I'm the woman to give them to him."

Anna ignored the invisible knife that pierced her. There was no way this woman knew she was incapable of having children, so she waited for the real reason behind the confrontation. Marybeth stepped closer. "He wants grandchildren with the right blood flowing through them. I come from the right family. I'm the one Thomas Bennett wants his son to marry."

Meeting the woman's gaze, Anna held her ground. "Has anyone asked Lucas what he wants?"

A cold smile flickered. "Lucas wants reconciliation with his father. Which woman do you think his having a relationship with is going to help further that?"

Sighing, not in the mood for this, Anna waved a hand. "Look Marybeth, I've got better things to do than fight over Lucas. He's a big boy and can take care of himself…and his father. I'll leave that to him. You've got no worries from me right now." Especially since her plan included not seeing Lucas anytime in the near future. He might wind up hating her, but at least he would be alive.

Surprise danced across Marybeth's features and she backed up a step, as though Anna had completely taken her aback, sucking the wind from her sails. "Well—" she cleared her throat "—I'm glad that's settled."

"Glad what's settled?" Lucas stepped from the kitchen into the foyer.

Startled, the women turned to face him. Marybeth immediately pasted a smile on her perfectly made-up face. "Nothing, darling, just girl stuff."

Anna felt the hurt run through her, not because of the smile Lucas sent back to the woman, but because of the fact she was going to have to leave him just when Lucas had started showing interest in becoming a Christian, and was opening himself up to the Lord. Which would allow the possibility of a relationship beyond friendship for the two of them.

Only he wanted children and she couldn't give him that. She silently warned herself not to forget that. As if. She smiled weakly at them and said, "I'll just be upstairs." Packing.

Without another word or a backward glance, she hurried up the stairs to her room.

And stopped. The door to her bedroom was cracked. She'd left it shut.

Had Maddy gone in to clean and straighten up even after she'd left the woman explicit instructions not to? Not that she had anything to hide, but old habits died hard. She didn't want anyone in her space. And someone had been in it—or still was.

Nerves tingling, the latest incident fresh in her mind, she wasn't taking any chances. Her breath coming a little faster, with the palm of her right hand, she slowly pushed the door inward, almost expecting to feel a bullet slam into her. Memories of the shooting just outside the FBI office rushed over her. She shoved them away, forced aside the paralyzing fear and held tight to her courage as she silently prayed for strength. Yes, Lucas was still downstairs, but if she called to him, whoever was in there would either get away or hurt someone in the process.

Assuming there was someone in there. And from the way her life had been going lately, she was going on that assumption. The door inched inward. Wishing she had

her gun or some kind of weapon, Anna stepped inside,
her gaze sweeping the room.

Empty.

But the closet door was closed and she knew for a
fact that she'd left it open.

ELEVEN

Lucas got rid of Marybeth as quickly as he could. He wasn't stupid. His father's plan for him to get involved with the woman simply because of her family background was just plain idiocy in his opinion. When he married, he'd marry for love.

Immediately, Anna's beautiful face appeared in his mind's eye. He gulped. Did he love her? Shoving that thought aside, not yet ready to analyze the intense feelings he had for the woman who kept trying to push him out of her life, he decided to call Mark and check on Paulo.

Mark answered on the fourth ring. "Hey Lucas, what's up?"

The wonders of caller ID. Smiling to himself, he asked, "How's my boy, Paulo?"

"Doing pretty well. Having that woman, Ella, with him really seems to lift his spirits. He likes her and she's great with him."

"Yeah, she's great, really, really great, isn't she? Yeah, she is."

"What's on your mind, friend?"

Lucas cleared his throat. "What do you mean?"

"Because you called me but aren't paying attention to me." A pause. "Ah, I get it. So, how's Anna?"

Feeling transparent, Lucas asked, "Have you ever been in love?"

Silence. Then, "Whoa, seriously? You think you love her?"

"Nah. Well, maybe. Ah, man, I don't know. She makes me crazy, though."

"Although, now that you say that, it all makes sense."

"What does?"

"Yeah, you've definitely got it bad. I mean, you followed her all the way back here from Brazil, right?"

"Hey, you know that was for Paulo," he protested.

Mark laughed. "Keep telling yourself that."

It stunned him to realize Mark was right. He'd followed a woman home. More than just home—he followed her all the way to another country. Oh, he wrapped it up in a good excuse. Anna needed to come as guardian. He needed to be here as Paulo's doctor. But the truth remained. He'd come with hopes of developing something more with Anna. He'd never done anything like that before in his life, had in fact, spent most of his time *running from* women. Now he was on the other side of the spectrum and it scared him to realize how much she meant to him. But as the idea sank in, it warmed his heart. The more he wanted to see her, to keep her safe, to be with her—and only her.

"One more thing," Lucas said. "You're a Christian, right?"

"You know it."

"I just wanted to say thanks for living your faith back in college. I didn't understand it back then, but I respected it."

"So, what are saying?" Suppressed excitement lent an edge to Mark's voice.

"I'm saying I think I understand it now."

"Do we need to talk?"

"Nope, let's just say, I believe, okay?"

Mark's joyous whoop through the phone line caused Lucas to grin. He thought about Anna, Paulo and Mark. They were living, practicing examples of faith, what it meant to follow God. He wanted his name added to that list. He thought about the tract, the simple prayer at the end. And knew what he was going to do. Peace flooded his entire being.

"Hey, Mark, thanks, and you're right about Anna. I owe you, but I gotta go."

Lucas had probably confused the poor man to death, jumping from topic to topic like he'd just done, but the sound of Mark's laughter still ringing in his ear after he hung up the phone told him his friend would survive. Lucas turned and started up the steps to see if Anna wanted to go grab a bite to eat—and have a heart-to-heart chat.

Anna moved closer to the closet, stopping by the nightstand to pull the heavy lamp from the surface. Not as effective as a gun, but at least it was something. She crept to the closet, placed her hand on the knob, and took a deep breath that did absolutely nothing to dispel the breathless feeling from her chest.

"What are you doing?"

The whisper sent her spinning toward the door, her heart in her throat, barely blocking the scream threatening to come out.

Lucas stood there, a frown on his face, his body tense as though ready to spring to her aid.

She shot him a fierce scowl and held a finger to her lips. With a nod of her head, she indicated the closet door.

He moved slowly inside the bedroom, sidling over to the closet. Soundless, he gave a little wave of his fingers asking her to hand over the lamp. She did, deciding it might be better for him to clobber anyone who might appear. He had a few more muscles than she did.

Thankful that he was willing to wait to ask all the questions swarming in his eyes, she reached once again for the knob.

And flung the door open.

Nothing.

Adrenaline still surging, it took her a moment to register that the space was empty. He lowered the lamp as she moved to the bed and yanked the bed skirt up.

Again, nothing.

The bathroom. Holding up a hand to forestall any questions, she soft-stepped it over to the bath. The shower curtain was still pulled back to the end of the rod, and the small linen closet she'd left open had been shut, but no one could hide in there.

She opened it anyway.

Towels and toiletries mocked her paranoia.

"What did you expect to find?" Lucas sounded concerned, not like she'd lost her mind concerned, just concerned. He'd been too involved in everything going on lately not to understand if she acted a little paranoid.

"Someone's been in here."

"What makes you think so?"

She told him about the doors. "I always leave things a certain way, so I know if…" She shrugged.

"So you'll know if something's out of place," he finished for her.

"Right."

"Anything else seem touched?"

Her eyes landed on her backpack shoved into the corner under the window. It looked undisturbed. Her small suitcase however, was unzipped. "Someone's been in my suitcase."

"You're sure?"

She shot him an exasperated look and didn't bother to answer as she crossed the room to inspect it. "It's partially unzipped, more so than I left it before our impromptu swim and subsequent hospital stay. I always rezip it until I get to the middle of this side." As she explained, she rummaged through it. All of her clothes seemed rumpled, but her personal documents were still in their little bag, documents that included her passport, a couple of credit cards and her medical information such as blood type, medical history, etc. should she have some type of emergency. The bag looked like it had been rummaged through, but nothing appeared to be missing.

Anna shrugged. "Maybe someone in your household wanted to get information on me for some reason."

Lucas ran a hand through his hair, obviously disgruntled. "Or maybe someone was looking for information to give to the doctor yesterday. Other than that I can't think of anyone who'd have a reason to search your belongings. Let's ask Maddy if she was in here, before we start looking for a suspect with suspicious motives."

Anna nodded and Lucas went to find Maddy.

While he was gone, she straightened the suitcase, went through each and every item but found nothing missing. Her backpack hadn't been touched, which she thought was odd. Maybe the intruder had been interrupted.

A sound at the door brought her attention around to see Lucas and Maddy coming back her way.

Lucas said, "Maddy says she hasn't been in here."

The woman looked worried, twisting her hands into knots before releasing them to repeat the gesture again. "I promise, miss, I haven't even been on this floor today. I've been helping in the kitchen like I always do on Thursdays because it's Cook's day off."

Anna searched Maddy's face and found no hint of deception. She offered a smile. "I believe you."

Relief showed clearly on her face and her hands relaxed. "Thank you. I really can't afford to lose this job."

"You don't have to worry about that," Anna hastened to reassure her, "but can you tell me if any staff has been in here? Or anyone who might have been in the house yesterday or this morning?"

A frown marked her forehead. "No, we had the heating and air conditioning man here because we had some problems with a rodent in the system. The creature must have fallen down the vent and couldn't get out." She shuddered then shrugged. "But other than the exterminators, there's only been the usual comings and goings."

"Maddy, do you mind asking if maybe Dahlia or Godfrey went through Anna's things to see if she might have needed something for the hospital stay?" Maddy agreed and left. He looked at Anna. "I know you had benefits through the orphanage, maybe one of them was looking the paperwork."

"Maybe, but why wouldn't they have said something at the hospital?" She didn't believe the flimsy explanation. And neither did Lucas if his expression was anything to go by. But he was grasping at straws, horrified to think the security of his father's house had been breached once again.

* * *

Questioning the staff and other household residents turned up nothing. No one could think of why anyone would be in Anna's room and no one had even thought to go through Anna's personal belongings to look for papers for the hospital. Lucas's father, a golfing buddy to the hospital chief of staff, had just assured them he would pay for anything needed.

Lucas paced the sunroom while Anna stood looking out to the ocean below. Her reflection in the glass was such that he could plainly see her face. "What are you thinking?"

She smiled but didn't turn. "You mean you don't know?"

"Probably something stupid like it's time for you to leave."

"Actually, yes. But even before leaving the hospital, I was thinking I…we…need help."

Grateful she'd included him in the thought, he walked up behind her and placed his hands on her shoulders. She leaned back against him and he relished the trust, the feel of her so close—and yet emotionally she was a long way away. He breathed against her ear, "I don't want you to leave."

She turned, looked up at him, her beauty taking his breath away. The sad smile that crossed her lips hurt him. "I don't want to leave you, Lucas. But I refuse to stay where you could get hurt. I've said it before, but I've not done much about it. Now, I think it's time to admit it's time for help. I'm going to ask a friend if she'll lend us her expertise."

"Who?" He moved back, unable to stay so close without pulling her into his arms. She looked bereft at his distance, but understanding, too. He stood next to her, shoving his hands in his pockets, looking out over the ocean.

"I've been racking my brain about who to ask for help other than Justin because, while I'm not sure he's guilty, I can't be one hundred percent sure he isn't. So, I've only come up with one possibility. Jennifer McDougall, a fellow FBI agent. We were actually partners once upon a time, but I haven't talked to her since I left. However, I'm sure she'd be more than willing to help me out if I ask. I also trust her."

"With your life?"

"With my life."

"Then why haven't you called her before now?"

Anna gave an almost invisible shudder, but Lucas caught the tremor. "Because it might mean putting her life in danger. Two FBI agents are already dead because of me and this case. How could I—" She broke off. "But now, I'm afraid since it was your car that was chosen in this latest attempt on my life that you might very well be a target, too. And even if I leave now, they'll still come after you simply because of your association with me. I can't just assume that if I'm gone, you're safe."

She'd really been analyzing this from every direction. Lucas rubbed his jaw, thinking. "So what's your plan? If you don't intend to sneak out in the middle of the night."

"No." She shook her head. "No sneaking. We need to be smart. Proactive."

"You have something in mind, don't you?"

Blowing out a breath, she nodded. "I'm going to that party at de Chastelain's house."

"What party?"

Slipping her hand into her pocket, she pulled out a

paper and thrust it at him. He read the invitation. "Won't he recognize you?"

"I really don't think so. I look a lot different than I did four years ago, plus, I'm going to be disguised as part of the catering crew. Trust me, the man won't look at me twice. Hired help is not worth his time or attention."

Lucas raked a hand through his hair. "No way. This is all just too crazy. There's got to be a better, safer way." He paced the length of the room and back. How could he get her to see reason? A quick look at her face told him he probably wouldn't have any luck. But he had to try. "What can I say to talk you out of this?"

Her chin jutted. "Nothing."

Closing his eyes, he sighed. "I was afraid of that. So what can I do to help?"

"Nothing. I'm going to call Jennifer and see if she can get me some information on the catering company. Like who's doing it and what their uniforms look like."

"What's your plan once you get inside?"

"To slip into de Chastelain's office and have a look around. That memory card didn't just walk off. The FBI raided the house really quickly after I called them. De Chastelain was too busy getting rid of the body and any evidence that he'd killed someone to have time to look for anything I might have hidden—even if he'd suspected I'd done so. The crime-scene people found a minimal amount of blood in the room, not enough to prove someone bled out there. Which isn't surprising since de Chastelain stabbed the man. I'm sure he had the rug removed and replaced it with one from one of the other rooms. The blood that was found was on the edge of the bottom of the sofa. When questioned about it, de Chastelain claimed he had had a nosebleed and must not have gotten it all cleaned up."

"Yeah, but blood typing could easily disprove that claim."

"True, but the blood type matched his. So did the DNA." She shrugged. "When that came back they didn't have justification for further investigation. They had no body, the blood type matched a man who was alive and well and de Chastelain was threatening to pull out the big guns with lawyers and such. So, the FBI backed off, especially since they didn't find that memory card I told them about."

"And you think you can find it after all this time? That seems unlikely."

"I have no idea. I just know I have to try to do something, find out a reason for it disappearing."

"You realize I'm going with you."

"Absolutely not." Twin lines appeared above her nose as she shot him a ferocious frown. "De Chastelain obviously knows by now that we know each other. If you show up, he's going to wonder why. It might make him suspicious enough to keep an eye out for me. And I definitely don't need that complication." Another thought made her gasp. "In fact, that very invitation could be a trap if he thinks you'll show up. De Chastelain isn't stupid. If he's been watching us like I think he has, then he probably realizes he could use you to get to me. I need you to stay here."

Storm clouds gathered in his eyes. "You aren't going alone. Forget it."

"I don't plan to go alone. That's where Jennifer comes in."

TWELVE

Sunday morning Anna came down the steps, stomach rumbling. It had been a long night and she'd not slept well. Tantalizing aromas greeted her as she entered the kitchen. Once she'd finally fallen asleep, she'd slept later than she'd intended and it looked like everyone else had finished up some time ago.

Except the man sitting at the table sipping his coffee, reading the newspaper. Oh boy. Did she turn and run or follow through on her original plans to satisfy her complaining stomach?

The decision made her pause for a split second. Long enough for Thomas Bennett to turn and scowl at her. "Well, are you waiting for an invitation?"

"No sir, not at all."

"Grab a plate and sit."

Part of her wanted to refuse based on the principle that no one bossed her around, but her midsection protested the thought by emitting another embarrassingly loud growl. "Thank you," she said stiffly. "I think I will."

She filled her plate from the small buffet table off to the side and sat in the chair farthest away from the cantankerous old man. Where was Lucas?

Maddy came in with a coffeepot and filled her cup for her. "Thank you, Maddy."

"You're welcome."

"Where is everyone?"

"Lucas said to let you sleep as long as you wanted. He decided to take one of the boats out for a spin. Godfrey and Dahlia decided to go away for a couple of days on a little minivacation."

"Yeah, now that you and Lucas are here, he figures you'll do to play babysitter." The bitter words couldn't quite hide the hint of resignation, as if Thomas had come to terms with the fact that he didn't like having to rely on someone else to make sure he was all right, but wasn't going to deny that he needed it. Maddy scurried out of the kitchen, intimidated by the man's tone.

Anna didn't let it bother her. She'd certainly dealt with worse when she'd been an agent. "Is there anything I can do for you?"

He gave her a speculative look. "No, there's nothing you can do for me that I can't do for myself in spite of what my nephew thinks."

Anna smiled. "I think you're a very clever man who knows how to get what he wants while making others believe that's what they want too."

Respect flickered in his eyes and he lifted his coffee cup in a sharp salute. "I'd say you are an extremely bright young woman."

"Hmm." She stabbed a bite of eggs and hid her surprise at the unexpected compliment. "I thought I might go to church. Is there one around here?"

"Church. What a crutch. You ought to learn to stand on your own two feet without needing all that religious stuff." He snorted. "And here I was thinking there was something I could respect about you. I thought you were a stronger woman than that."

Anna considered how to respond. She'd noticed the hurt beneath the bluster, so she went the soft but firm route. "I'm strong because of Him." She leaned forward. "Tell me something. Why is it so wrong to ask for help? When you're sick, don't you go to the doctor? When your car breaks down, don't you take it to the person who can fix it? Why is it so wrong to turn to God when you need strength in your spirit, your soul?"

That stopped him a moment. He opened his mouth to say something, then snapped it shut. Opened it again. Shut it again.

Anna laid a hand over his, compassion stirring her. "I don't know why you're so angry and bitter with God, whether it's because of Lance's death or your wife's, or something altogether unrelated to that, but God's big enough to handle it. Maybe you should talk to Him about it. Give Him a chance to help you deal with it."

She'd stumped the poor man. He looked absolutely lost for words. Anna gave him another gentle smile and quietly finished her breakfast.

Thomas continued to sip his coffee and read his paper, but every once in a while Anna would feel his gaze on her. She waited.

Clearing his throat, the man finally asked, "So, you're the reason my boy is thinking about religion? God?"

"I think God is the reason Lucas is thinking about God. But I hope that I was able to influence him in that direction."

"Humph."

Giving him another smile, she got to her feet and left the room. She was hoping Lucas was back so she could ask him to go to church with her. He was and agreed to go with her.

Two hours later, the service over, they stepped out of the old church building with Anna's heart feeling more peaceful than it had in a long time. Part of that had to do with the fact that Lucas had joined her and said he'd enjoyed the service. He'd changed since Paulo's surgery and the day in the ocean. His eyes held a new sense of contentment. Yes, she still had a killer after her and Lucas was trapped right in the middle, but the knowledge that God was on their side brought them both a confidence that she couldn't deny. Her heart rejoiced in his newfound faith. She just prayed she'd have the chance to watch him grow in it.

Anna knew the service had been just what she needed even though she'd looked over her shoulder more than once. She couldn't shake that creepy feeling of being watched. Still, the worship music had been wonderful and the pastor had a straight-to-the-point sermon on living your faith, being an example to those around you. Anna had prayed for another opportunity to do that again with Lucas's father.

However, the chance never popped up because all week long Anna laid low, rarely leaving the house, staying more to herself or spending time with Lucas rather than being social. She'd also seriously considered leaving again, but finally gave up the idea because every time she suggested the possibility, Lucas vetoed it with promises to track her down. For his own safety, she stayed, assuring herself the relief she felt at not leaving had nothing to do with the fact that she didn't want to leave Lucas, but that she wouldn't have to find a cheap hotel room to hole up in.

The fact that Lucas had called in a couple of favors and had someone watching the house around the clock also helped her in making the decision. He waved off her protest at the expense he was incurring and she finally gave in, admitting she felt safer in spite of her objections. So, Andrew Silver had arrived, a man of medium height, steely muscles and a subdued demeanor. She didn't let that fool her. He would be lethal in a fight. Lucas had decided to hire the man for extra protection after the break-in of her room last week, which had made him nervous, and she'd agreed to the need for the tighter security—at least until she left.

Andrew stayed back, out of sight but always watching. Lucas and Andrew had gone to college together and remained friends even when their careers took off in different directions. He'd been glad to catch up with Lucas and appreciated the job.

She checked on Paulo's progress daily and was ecstatic to hear how quickly the little guy was recuperating. Their talks on the phone were the highlight of her day, other than when she and Lucas managed to spend some time together.

Marybeth Ferris showed up for dinner nearly every day and when she did, Anna took most of her meals in her room, not wanting to bother with the woman's jealousy. Plus, she didn't want to hear from Thomas Bennett how Marybeth was the perfect mother for his grandchildren.

Nope, she'd just save herself some grief and do the cowardly thing by hiding out and avoiding the situation. She did join Lucas and rest of the family for Thanksgiving dinner, but otherwise, she kept to herself as much as possible.

And worked on the plan to get into de Chastelain's house.

Jennifer had been thrilled to hear from her, but shocked when Anna revealed her suspicions about Justin. Promising to look into Justin, Jennifer also agreed to get a catering uniform for Anna and have it sent to the Bennett house.

It had arrived thirty minutes ago. The party was tomorrow night.

She'd tried on the uniform of black shoes, black pants, a white long-sleeved tuxedo shirt with a black bow tie and a maroon button-up vest. Her hair, the curls long enough now to be pulled into a short ponytail, would be gathered up into a hairnet. And her ensemble would be complete.

The knock on the door pulled her away from the mirror. That would be Lucas.

Pausing, her hand on the knob, her heart galloping full speed ahead at the idea of spending time with Lucas, she told her pulse to settle down. A deep breath helped settle her nerves and she pulled the door open.

And the butterflies moved in. Nuts.

Ignoring her fluttering stomach, she smiled.

"How'd you like to do something a little different today?" he asked.

"What?"

"What if I took you flying?"

"Flying? As in wings and in the air?"

He chuckled. "Yeah, I think we could both use a stress reliever. I called Ted and asked him to get the plane ready."

"You own a plane?"

"Well, not me, personally. It's Ted's plane. His passion. But he taught me to fly before I could drive, and I've kept my license current. So, are you up to it?"

She hesitated. A whole week had passed without incident, yet she had the gloomy feeling of waiting for the other shoe to fall. Did she dare hope they could go flying without something going wrong?

"Come on." He took her hand in his and she allowed him to pull her from the room. She pushed aside the negative feelings, instead focusing on noticing how nicely his large palm wrapped around her fingers. She followed him down to the small hangar she'd thought was just a fancy barn.

Ted and Joni lived in the house next to the hangar. "So, Ted knows how to fly a plane."

"And anything else with wings."

Anna pulled to a stop. "Does he know how to fly a helicopter?"

"Sure…" Lucas trailed off, seeing where she was going with this line of questioning. He held up his hands. "No way. Don't even go thinking that Ted had anything to do with that business out on the ocean. He's been with my family for years. Actually, I think of Ted as more of a father than I do my own flesh and blood."

"I'm not accusing him, Lucas, just asking."

"And I'm telling you to forget it," he snapped.

Slapping her hands on her hips, she said, "And I'm telling you, I have to investigate every angle."

Drawing in a deep breath, Lucas shut his eyes briefly. When he opened them, most of his initial defensiveness was gone. "I'm sorry. It's just…I can't even comprehend…"

"This is going to sound awful, but I'm going to ask. What is Ted's financial status? Could he be bought off? I mean, think about it. He's had access to everything. He's a pilot. He had access to your car at the hospital. He knew we were coming home from the airport. He could search my room with no one thinking anything about him being in the house. He also had time to be picked up by the boat, get back to the house, change clothes, grab another boat and come get us. Everything, Lucas. It all fits."

"Maybe it fits too easily."

"Or maybe it fits just right."

"But how would de Chastelain know you and I were flying back from Brazil?"

"Justin. What if Justin told him I flew home with you?"

A light dawned as he followed her logic. His face lost a few shades of color as he played it out. "So Justin calls de Chastelain to warn him. De Chastelain does a little investigation into my father's staff to see who might be bought off. Finds something on Ted and blackmails him into setting up all these incidences. Then Ted has a change of heart at the last minute and rescues us from the ocean, or simply rescues us to throw suspicion away from himself. Maybe de Chastelain threatened him with something, violence against his family, or whatever and Ted cut the brakes to the car after he helped deliver it to the hospital."

"Could it be?" she whispered.

"Maybe instead of going flying, we need to do a little investigating into Ted's background."

THIRTEEN

While Andrew, Lucas's friend/bodyguard checked into Ted's background, Lucas waited for Anna to finish getting ready for de Chastelain's party. She didn't want him going, but that was just too bad. He understood her reasons for not wanting him there, but he'd skulk around outside if he had to, because there was no way he was going to let her do this alone.

Finally, she appeared at the top of the steps and his heart tripped all over itself to make her proud by beating just for her.

"Good heavens, what on earth are you doing dressed like the help?"

Lucas turned in the direction of the disdainful voice and said, "Just think of it as a costume party, Father."

The man sniffed, "Surely she could have come up with a better costume than…that." He waved a gnarled hand toward Anna, who merely smiled and gracefully descended the stairs, saying, "Hello, Mr. Bennett. I hope you have a lovely evening. Will you be joining us for church in the morning?"

The man snorted, "Not likely, although I'm sure Lucas will put in an appearance since he's gone and got religion now." Muttering under his breath as he moved toward his parlor, he shuffled past Lucas, who caught the words, "Someone who floats down the stairs should be dressed in silk for a ball, not bartending."

Anna grinned up at him from the bottom step, the stress of what she was about to do disappearing from her features for a brief moment. "It's a catering uniform, sir." The man ignored her as continued on into the other room. She transferred her grin to Lucas. "I do believe he just paid me a compliment."

Lucas reached out and pulled her to him. "He's right, you know."

She quirked an eyebrow.

"You float. You're very beautiful even dressed like a bartender, and I'm scared to death something's going to happen to you."

"Nothing's going to happen as long as I'm very careful. Jennifer will be outside able to hear every word I say thanks to this handy-dandy little earpiece and microphone. She's talked a few other fellow agents into coming, too, just in case." Reaching up, she gave it a gentle tap. "If I get into trouble, I just have to give her the signal and she'll have FBI swarming all over the place." She frowned, just seeming to notice him dressed in a tux. Attraction flared in her eyes for a brief moment before suspicion drew her delicate eyebrows down toward the bridge of her nose. "Why do you have on a tux?"

"I'm going with you."

"Lucas, I've already told you…" He cut her off with a finger over her lips. He'd think about their warmth later.

"I've come prepared," he said. "Look."

He reached into his jacket pocket and pulled out a pair of black-rimmed glasses. A set of false teeth changed the shape of his mouth and a black wig that looked as real as his own hair covered his head. Freshly shaven, there wasn't a blond whisker to give him away. He pulled one more item from his pocket and pressed a neatly trimmed, wig-matching goatee to his chin. His eyebrows were dark enough to pass muster without dying them. He looked like an entirely different person.

"Where did you get this stuff?"

"I called Jennifer and asked her to help me out."

Anna rolled her eyes, mentally reminding herself to have a talk with her friend. However, right now she had a party to get to and if he was determined to go with her…

"All right, but stay as inconspicuous as possible and don't act like you know me. Deal?"

His eyes lit up. "Deal."

She frowned again. "This isn't a game, Lucas."

Immediately serious, he said, "I'm well aware of that fact. Your safety is the most important thing in the world to me right now. You don't have to remind me how dangerous this is. In fact, I've already appealed to God for your safety."

"Really?"

"Yes." He left it at that but she shot him a look that said he would be doing some explaining in the near future.

Sucking in a deep breath, she nodded. "Okay. Then let's get going."

Two hours later, they pulled up to the gate. Anna had wrapped a faux-fur coat around her to hide her uniform from the guard. Out of the corner of her eye, she caught sight of Jennifer in the driver's seat of one of the many news vans.

She laughed to herself. Great thinking, Jennifer. The media was all over this party, hoping for a way in or at least an exclusive interview with one of the guests. No one would ever suspect the woman was an agent on a mission. Lucas flashed the invitation and they were on their way up the driveway to the mansion she'd never wanted to see again.

Memories assailed her as the house came into sight. Beautifully decorated for Christmas, with wreaths hanging and candles winking from every window, the house glowed with warmth and good cheer. A fully decorated Christmas tree stood on each end of the massive wraparound porch. Anna knew the welcoming appearance was merely an illusion; that underneath it all, behind the double oak door, lay evil and death. She shuddered, wishing she could turn around and go back into hiding…take the easy way out, cave in to the fear stuttering through her.

"You okay?"

Lucas's quiet question intruded on her flashbacks. She nodded and shoved away the memories along with her panic. "Yeah." Then she spoke to the air. "Jennifer, can you hear me okay?"

"Loud and clear. You be careful in there." Jennifer's voice came through her tiny earpiece.

"Right."

Lucas pulled the car up to the front door, stepped out and came around to let her out. She snuggled into the fur, shivering in the cold night air as Lucas handed the valet parking attendant his key and a tip.

The man sped off and as soon as the second attendant was busy with the guests arriving next, she and Lucas slipped into the shadows to slink around to the side of the house. Anna made her way to the kitchen entrance. The catering truck was backed up to the door, but no one was around. They'd probably already finished unloading. Hopefully, she'd be able to blend in if she kept her head low and didn't make any eye contact. Lucas grabbed her arm before she could enter. "Are you sure about this?"

Shivering, she stared up into his concerned eyes and knew that concern was for her. Heart clenching, she stepped in close to wrap him in a hug, breathing in his clean, masculine scent. "I'm sure. All I need to do is slip into the office, look around. I'm not planning on lingering. In and out, I promise. If I find something, I'll call in the troops. If not…"

"But—"

"Here." She cut him off and shrugged out of the coat. "I won't be needing this."

Lucas caught her hand. "Say a prayer."

Startled, she paused. "What?"

"Just say a prayer. You're not going into this without being covered in prayer."

"Wow," she whispered.

"We'll talk later. Now pray."

She did, then stepped back, looked into his eyes and felt a sweet relief move through her soul. Lucas had definitely made his peace with God.

Smoothing her hands down the sides of her freshly starched black pants, she threw her shoulders back and clipped her hair up into the net. She was ready. She warned him, "Don't get caught out here. Everyone's on the other side of the house where the large den and dining room are. There's also a huge glassed-in terrace that wraps halfway around the house. A lot of people will be out there." She paused, took a deep breath then said, "All right, Jenn, just like old times, hey girl? Showtime, my friend."

"Back atcha," came the response in her left ear.

With one last look at a worried Lucas, Anna twisted the knob and slipped into the kitchen.

FOURTEEN

Lucas figured he was intimately familiar with stress. Look at the family he came from, the job he'd held the past three years, the fact that someone was trying to kill Anna and might just get him in the process. Yes, he knew stress, but watching her disappear into the kitchen of the man who wanted her dead just about did him in. His gut was in a permanent clench, and he figured he had a good start on an ulcer.

But he couldn't just stand there like a coat rack holding the fur. Tossing the item over the nearest bush, he straightened his tux and did his best to imitate a man simply out for a stroll.

As he made progress around the perimeter of the house, the noise from the terrace reached him. But it was de Chastelain that Lucas wanted to keep an eye on. He gave a tug on the itchy wig, shifted the teeth in his mouth and slipped on the glasses.

Now that he had the chance to study it, the house took his breath away. Magnificently built, the entire back side was glass, to give the viewer a splendid view of the ocean down below—and, for someone standing out in the dark, a perfect view of the happenings inside the brilliantly lit home. He could literally see into three rooms at once.

He looked for Anna but wasn't able to spot her. Sticking to the shadows, he moved on down to see a different section of the crowd—and nearly dropped his false teeth when he realized he was staring into the face of Shawn de Chastelain.

Fortunately, the man was laughing at something one of his guests had said and didn't realize he was being watched. Then from the corner of Lucas's eye, Anna came into view. Her head low, she held a tray bearing all kinds of professionally concocted treats. Several people reached to take one off the tray, but didn't appear to notice the person holding it.

With lithe grace, she weaved her way through the mass of humanity, her goal the stairs. As Lucas kept his eyes on her, he moved parallel to her movements. Looking back, he breathed a small sigh of relief to note that de Chastelain seemed oblivious to Anna.

Still she moved with agility, stopping every once in a while to allow a guest to sample one of the pastries on her tray, then she was on the move again, her goal the door down the hall to her left. She'd described the layout of the house to him, but now, from this perspective, he understood her explanation a little better. Just a few more steps and she'd be in front of de Chastelain's office door.

Anna balanced the tray expertly, her years of waitressing in college coming back into play. She was almost there. Her eyes scanned the room, searching for de Chastelain. Good. He was engrossed in something someone was saying. She did wish he'd turn around and put his back to her, but as long as he wasn't paying attention…

Setting the tray on a table near the office door, she moved closer to it, waiting for her chance. She scanned the crowd and managed to keep de Chastelain in her sight at all times. De Chastelain's wife, Sherry, crossed the room to her husband's side, twined her arm through de Chastelain's and smirked at the pretty, petite guest who'd captured his attention. The young woman flinched, covered it with a demure smile…and slunk away.

Poor Sherry, Anna thought. She had a sham of a marriage and no assurance of a husband who loved her and was faithful. In fact, she knew otherwise. While Anna had worked there, it had been a topic of many heated arguments. Yet, Sherry stayed with him. The whole scenario made Anna sad and showed her exactly what she didn't want in a marriage.

Finally, a rather large woman crossed in front of de Chastelain. Tossing away thoughts of de Chastelain and Sherry, Anna focused on the job she was there to do, and twisted the knob to slip inside the office.

Heart pounding, breath whistling in short gasps, she realized her nerves were going to need some major reconstruction after this adventure…assuming she made it out without being caught. She studied the room that looked almost exactly like it had four years ago. De Chastelain's wife had changed nothing. Excitement leaped within her. Touches of Christmas cheer mocked her. A small tree on the desk blinked its multicolored lights and mistletoe hung from the light fixture in the center of the room.

And the umbrella stand stood right where it had the night of the murder. Upon closer inspection, she realized the desk was different, a close copy, but different. Somehow, de Chastelain had managed to switch the desks. Then she remembered this one as being the desk from the upstairs study. And, most likely, had no little secret drawer.

Crossing to the umbrella stand, she pulled out the decorative arrangement and set it aside. Then she picked up the stand and turned it upside down, fully expecting the memory card to fall out with a clink.

Nothing.

Frustration nearly choked her. Think. Think. She scanned the floor, the beautiful hardwood, the new area rug that hadn't been there four years ago. Bending to her knees, she pulled up the edge—and froze.

The creature must have fallen down the vent and couldn't get out. Maddy's words echoed in her head as she stared at the air-conditioning vent located only a couple of inches from the umbrella stand. *The creature must have fallen down the vent and couldn't get out.*

Could it be?

A sound at the door swung her around. Quickly, she picked the arrangement up and stuffed it back where it belonged. She rolled the rug back over the vent and froze, huddling behind the desk.

Giggling and shushes filtered their way through the closed door and footsteps made their way on down the hall. Anna nearly wilted with relief. She honestly had no idea what she would say if she was caught.

No time to think up a story. She'd have to be creative if the need arose.

Immediately turning her attention back to the rug, she pulled it up again. Grateful, she'd thought to bring a small penlight, she snatched it from her back pocket, knelt on the floor and shone the beam into the vent.

And there it was. The memory card, caught in a cobweb suspended in the shaft, illuminated by the thin stream of light, blinked sleepily up at her as though offended by the intrusion after all these years.

Pure, unadulterated disbelief made her voice shaky. "Jenn, I found it."

"You're kidding."

"It's here."

"Good, now leave it and get out so we can find a reason to get a search warrant."

"I can't get to it," she ground out, ignoring Jenn's order. Excitement warred with frustration. So close, so close. She'd have to pry the vent off then find a safer place to stash it. She didn't want to leave it hanging on that web a moment longer in spite of the fact that it had been there for four years.

Jennifer's voice hardened. "Well, I can't send anyone in. I don't have just cause to search the man's house. I need you to get out and help me find a reason. Then we'll get the card."

The door opened and once again, Anna froze.

"Anna, you in here?" the voice whispered.

Lucas.

How much more adrenaline could her body produce? Her heart still pounding, not bothering to rise to her feet, she looked up over the edge of the desk and did a double take at his altered appearance.

"What are you doing in here?" she whispered. "Are you crazy?"

She didn't have time for this. Pulling open the desk drawer, she searched for something, anything to lift the vent. A nail file, a screwdriver. If she could get the cover off, she could reach down there and grab the card.

But she would only get one chance. If she knocked it loose, they'd have to take apart the system to get to it, as it would slide on down into the shaft.

She slid the drawer shut and tried the next one.

"De Chastelain kept looking this way. I managed to slip in when he turned to talk to another guest, but my guess is he's getting ready to come in here."

Anna groaned. "Not yet. I'm so close." Nothing in that drawer. She slid open the bottom one and found a metal ruler. It would do. Grabbing it, she jammed the thin edge up under the vent cover and lifted. It rose partially.

"Come on, Anna, you're making me nervous."

"Crack the door and see if you see him."

"Anna," Jennifer spoke into her ear. "I can hear everything. You need to get out of there if there's a chance de Chastelain is going to walk in on you."

"I'm not leaving without making sure that evidence isn't going to disappear…again." She had visions of the thing being jarred loose, sliding on down the vent and she'd have no way of proving she'd been right all these years. Not to mention that de Chastelain would get away with murder. And Lucas's life would still be in danger…because she failed. She had to get that card.

"It's been there four years, it's not going anywhere. Now get out."

Lucas came back from the door. "He's closer, definitely heading this way, but getting stopped along the way by people."

"I've. Almost. Got. It." The ruler snapped and Anna fell back with a growl of frustration.

He grabbed her hand, pulled her up, then stepped on the vent to squash it back into place. He rolled the rug back over it and grabbed up the broken ruler. Anna nearly screamed at him. Instead she lowered her voice and asked through gritted teeth, "What do you think you're doing?"

Gripping her cheeks, he forced her to look him in the eye, through the clear glass of the glasses into his beautiful brown ones. With one hand, he stuffed the ruler into his back pocket, then pulled the false teeth from his mouth and slid them in his front pocket. "You're not thinking clearly. What's going to happen if you tamper with that evidence?"

She stopped and closed her eyes. "I wasn't going to take it, just…move it. To a safer place." Her beautiful sapphire eyes popped back open to meet his.

He urged her, "Think, Anna. You can't do that."

Anxiety knit her eyebrows together. "But if it falls…"

"Then someone will go to a lot of trouble to get it, but it can't be you. Think it through. You'll do the very opposite of what you're working so hard to accomplish. You'll screw up the investigation and de Chastelain will get off on some technicality." He paused, his eyes twin beams of intensity. "You're always saying how God is in control. Well, trust Him. Do the right thing and exercise that faith of yours that I admire so much."

"Listen to him, Anna, he's right." Jennifer's no-nonsense tone startled her. Anna had forgotten about the woman.

The door opened and Lucas's lips swooped down to claim hers. Shocked, she jumped, then the kiss caught her attention to the exclusion of all else. She felt her lips soften, relished the feel of this man holding her in his arms.

The clearing of a throat pulled them apart. She buried

her face in Lucas's chest, knowing her face had to be flaming red. As she started to turn toward the newcomer, Lucas's palm trapped her head against him. She relaxed, getting the message. He didn't want whoever was in the doorway to see her face.

De Chastelain spoke. "Could you two take that somewhere else? This is my private office and I don't appreciate trespassers. Isn't she supposed to be working anyway?"

Lucas responded with a lisp. Somehow he'd managed to shove those awful teeth back in his mouth before looking at de Chastelain. "Yes, we were just taking advantage of the mistletoe, but no problem, we'll get right out."

"See to it." Someone called his name from behind and de Chastelain gave a growl of disgust, then Anna heard him say, "Out. Now."

The door shut and Anna sagged, Lucas's muscular arms the only thing keeping her from hitting the floor. He maneuvered her to the love seat to allow her to catch her breath.

"That was close," he muttered.

"Too close. I think I've come to my senses now." She slid him a shaky look, tried to relieve the tension by saying, "At least the ones you managed not to rattle with that kiss. But you're right. Let's get out of here before he decides to come back and give us a personal escort."

Just the thought of coming face-to-face with the man had her shuddering, reliving her past. All the feelings, emotions she'd felt that night she'd seen him kill a man swept through her, causing her to tremble uncontrollably. At least she blamed it on the memories and not the kiss that still tingled on her lips. She stood, forced her legs to walk to the door. What had that kiss meant to him? Did he feel what she felt? She vowed to ask him as soon as possible.

"Hey."

Lucas's soft whisper brought her attention back to him. He was staring at a picture that had fallen to the floor, no doubt thanks to her rustling through the desk.

"What is it?" She walked back over to him to peer over his shoulder.

Two boys about six years old stood side by side, an arm wrapped around each other's shoulders, identical smiles grinning for the camera.

"I think I know who your missing body is."

They made it back to Lucas's house without further incident with Lucas offering an explanation for the latest bombshell he'd just dropped on her. They were *twins*. Lucas explained that twins had identical DNA. There would be no way to know which brother the blood came from. The only thing that would differentiate the twins would be fingerprints.

Anna told Lucas, "The FBI had actually considered that Shawn and Brandon de Chastelain could be twins, but didn't find any evidence of it. We knew the boys had been born in Ireland, but had no idea in what city, and Shawn couldn't or wouldn't tell." She snorted. "He claims to have no memories of his life before foster care—and he sure wasn't going to spill the beans about being a twin, not having just committed a murder."

But as long as they couldn't find Brandon, they couldn't prove the blood wasn't Shawn's and couldn't convict him of said murder. "Justin did tell me that they'd contacted the authorities in several of the major cities in Ireland to see if they could turn up something on Brandon. But they came up empty, and they couldn't search the entire country."

Anna shrugged. "Who knows what the real story was? All we really know is that the boys were put into foster care and lousy records were kept. I wonder if their mother was even an American citizen—and if not, it was probably easy to slip through the cracks."

She thought about the photo of the two little boys, and her heart ached for all that lost innocence.

The picture hadn't been there when Anna had been in the house four years ago. She wondered if he'd put it there as a reminder. Some kind of penance for killing his brother? She'd been floored by the idea that the dead man was Brandon de Chastelain, but agreed that it wasn't a completely crazy theory. It would definitely explain why no one had been able to track him down. She had run the information by Jennifer, who'd promised to look into it and update them if she found anything.

Jennifer was also aware of the location of the memory card and would take the information back to her supervisor, agreeing to leave Justin out of the loop. The assistant District Attorney would request a search warrant based on Jennifer's report. Now all she and Lucas could do at this point was hurry up and wait. Jennifer promised to call as soon as everything went down.

With all that taken care of, Lucas was back to the decision of what to do about Ted. Anna sat on the sofa and he paced the floor, struggling to come to terms with what he'd found out about a man he'd trusted implicitly.

Thanks to the information provided by his friend/body-guard, Lucas now knew Ted was actually a former convict. In college, the man had been arrested for being involved in a plot to bomb an abortion clinic.

The information unsettled Lucas, but didn't really fit with the man trying to kill Anna—or the man who'd tried for years to get Lucas's family in church. It just didn't…match up. And Ted wasn't strapped financially. Nor did he seem to have any reason to accept a bribe or be subject to blackmail. Except for the incident in college. Had de Chastelain threatened to reveal this secret to the Bennett family unless Ted helped get rid of Anna?

"You know, Anna, even if de Chastelain had something on Ted, I just see Ted telling the man to do his worst, then coming to me about it." Even though all the evidence said, yes, to Ted's guilt, Lucas still didn't believe it.

The only way to take care of this was to ask the man.

Which is why he now found himself wearing out the rug in his father's office. The knock on the door had him taking a deep breath.

"Come in."

Ted entered, nodded a greeting to Anna then shut the door behind him. Concern glistened in his soft brown eyes and his hands played with the chauffeur's hat he enjoyed wearing. "What's going on, Lucas? You sounded strange on the phone."

Lucas ran a hand through his hair. This was one of the hardest things he'd ever done. "Will you tell me about the abortion clinic you were accused of trying to bomb?"

Surprise flickered then resignation took over. "Ah. What made you investigate my past?" Ted's tone was curious without being defensive.

"All the attempts being made on Anna's life. You came up as the most likely suspect."

Lucas explained what he and Anna had discussed, how they'd arrived at his name the day they'd almost gone flying.

Ted paced the floor, his right hand rubbing his five-o'clock shadow. "I'd hoped to leave the past in the past, but I guess I'm not surprised it's caught up with me." He shrugged. "In college, I got involved in a group that had a hidden agenda. Oh, I'm not saying I'm completely innocent. I did my share of protesting the clinics, arguing with the doctors, stepping up on my high horse. When they talked about bombing the clinic, though, I spoke up, told them they were crazy. I was ready to quit the entire organization and start one of my own. A peaceful one. But, that night, my roommate talked me into going to what was supposed to be our regular meeting. Just one last time, he promised. No violence, just talk. And it was a setup. They had bomb materials hidden in the house. Someone tipped off the police and the rest is history. I was guilty by association and served a short time in jail."

"Does my father know this?"

"Yes."

Lucas blinked. "Really?"

"He gave me a job when no one else would hire me—an ex-con. I'll always be grateful to him."

Well, that explained a lot. Like why Ted continued to stay on, and was so loyal to an irascible, cantankerous and even downright rude man.

Ted looked at Anna, who'd been silent during Ted's explanation. "I promise, Anna, I've not done anything to put you in harm's way."

Anna crossed to Ted and laid a hand on his arm. "I believe you."

Lucas gave the man a bear hug. "I do, too. I'm sorry I doubted you even for a minute."

Ted shrugged. "The evidence is certainly stacked against me, isn't it? Hearing you lay it all out certainly makes me stop and think. It's rather scary how much it looks like I could be a part of a plot to kill Anna."

"But obviously, things aren't as they appear," Anna muttered. "It's all like some weird illusion. You see one thing, but it's really another."

"Which means we need to keep digging to find the truth."

The next morning, Anna awoke to her cell phone buzzing. Fumbling around on the nightstand, she finally clamped her fingers around it and looked at the caller ID. Jennifer.

Did she have some news? Already?

"Hello?"

"Hi, Anna, thought you might like to know the ADA managed to finagle a warrant from Judge Bishop. We found your memory card."

Anna's breath left her in a whoosh. "And?"

"Everything you said was on it, was. Plenty to put de Chastelain away for a long time. I don't know that we'll be able to get him for murder without a body or a weapon. That small amount of blood could be explained by a nosebleed and the blood type did match de Chastelain's, but we've got drug transactions, names of some pretty high-ranking people involved in some nasty stuff. We're still looking for his brother, Brandon, but nothing's turned up on him."

"He's dead. De Chastelain knows where his body is—you'll just have to get him to talk. Offer him a deal or something."

A sigh whispered over the line. "It's possible. We're working on Sherry de Chastelain, too. I think that woman knows a lot more than she's telling. Our people are still working with the card, but de Chastelain has been arrested again so it looks like you're home free. Now…are you ready to come back to work?"

A fist in her stomach would have carried less of a punch than Jennifer's innocent question. Swallowing hard, Anna said, "No. Not yet. I need to know if you turn up something on Justin. I trusted him, Jennifer, with my life. If he's the reason those two agents are dead…"

"Yeah, I'm still working on it, but it looks like he's clean. I'll let you know if I find anything. Hey, you want to get together for some lunch tomorrow?"

"Sure, that sounds good." It did. It sounded wonderful. It took a moment to sink in. She'd done it. De Chastelain was in jail and Anna didn't have to look over her shoulder anymore. She wondered how long it would take for that reality to set in. "What time?"

"How about eleven-thirty at the steak house we used to haunt when we were partners a hundred years ago?"

The steak house. Wow, that would bring back some memories.

"See you there. Thanks." Anna hung up the phone, staring out the window to study the ocean as the waves lapped against the shore. The magnificent beauty of God's handiwork only briefly brushed her mind as she thought.

It was over.

It was really over. Finally, after four years, she'd helped to put the man behind bars, hopefully permanently this time. She did feel relief, gratitude that Lucas was now safe, but she also felt…unsettled, like she was missing something, something that might come back to haunt her if she didn't figure out what it was.

FIFTEEN

The next morning, she ate a quick breakfast and told Lucas she had some errands to run. He had some things of his own to take care of so he volunteered to drop her off at the steak house to eat with Jennifer while he did his own thing.

Anna took him up on the offer and a couple of hours later they made the drive in comfortable silence. Anna simply enjoyed being with him, yet the feeling was bittersweet as she knew it was time for her to leave, time for her to head back to the orphanage and take Paulo with her as soon as he was well enough. Which would be in a couple of weeks.

Lucas pulled up to the curb to let Anna out. She gave him a smile and said, "Thanks. Jennifer can bring me back to the house."

"You're sure?"

"I'm sure."

He shrugged. "I don't mind waiting for you."

"Thanks, Lucas, but I don't know how long I'll be, so don't wait around, okay?"

"Okay, see you back at the house."

She slammed the door. Lucas drove off and she turned to greet her friend. "Hey there."

Jennifer reached over and gave her a hug. "It's so good to do this again. Come on, I'm starved!"

"You're always hungry. I'm glad to see some things haven't changed."

"Ha-ha. Very funny."

"Before we set business aside, I just need to ask if the crime-scene guys got anything off the helicopter?"

Pursing her lips, Jennifer shook her head. "They've managed to recover some sort of serial number. I think it's only a matter of time before our people figure out who it belongs to. Not expecting the thing to crash, I'm sure they probably left some kind of evidence behind. We just have to find it."

Anna nodded. "Well, if you can put a rush job on it, I'd appreciate it."

Ten minutes later, they were seated at a table for two. Anna placed her napkin in her lap and took a sip of water. "So, what's been going on with you? We've been all business since I popped back into your life and we haven't had a chance to catch up."

"Life's pretty good, but I'm more interested in you." The food arrived and Jennifer took a bite of salad, asking, "So, how are things with you and Dr. Delicious?"

The sip of water Anna had just taken got stuck going down the wrong pipe and had her choking with gasping laughter again, but she managed, "Don't do that!" She took another deep breath and giggled. "Dr. Delicious? Oh please. Lucas would be mortified to hear you describe him that way."

"Sorry." An unrepentant grin said she was anything but.

Anna shrugged, turning serious. "He's a Christian now. God answered that prayer in a pretty crazy way, but the end result is Lucas realized he needs God."

"That's wonderful, Anna."

"Yes, it is." She toyed with the food on her plate, her appetite suddenly nonexistent.

"Um, so why do you say that like it's a bad thing?"

"Because that means there's nothing holding us back from exploring our feelings."

"And that's bad because…?"

Anna dropped her fork and looked her friend in the eye. "I can't have children, Jennifer, you know that."

"Yes, I do, but any man worth anything won't hold that against you. Not if he really loves you."

Tears came so easy when the topic of children came up. Anna sniffed them back, took a bite of food then wished she hadn't. Forcing herself to swallow, she blurted, "You know the FBI agents assigned to guard me while I was in the hospital?"

Jennifer blinked. "Yes."

"Do you know what one of them told me before he was killed? He said, 'Too bad about your hysterectomy. Not much good for any man now, are you?'"

Gasping, her eyes wide with horror at the crassness of somebody saying such a terrible thing, Jennifer reached across the table to grab Anna's hand. "You can't possibly believe that, can you?"

"I didn't think so, but for some reason his words keep going around and around in my head and I can't…" She looked away then back. "I love Lucas so much, I can admit that now. But what if I tell him everything and he looks at me…different? With…disgust or…"

"Then he's not the man for you." Anna felt her friend's hand grip hers even tighter. "You are a child of the King. He knit you in your mother's womb. He knows the plans He has for you. Plans to prosper you, never to harm you. That's a paraphrase, but you know the Bible. You know God loves you. I think God brought you and Lucas together for a purpose. It's all part of His plan. That man loves you. Tell him, Anna. I think you'll be surprised."

For the next two hours, Anna concentrated on her friend, the fact that it was wonderful not to have to look over her shoulder on a regular basis, and she forced all thoughts of Lucas and leaving him from her mind.

De Chastelain's arrest had once again captured the media's attention. Protesting his innocence all the way to jail, he vowed not to rest until he proved it. The authorities had rounded up several people in conjunction with a number of unsolved crimes. Their names had been on the memory card and they had various associations with de Chastelain. But the afternoon news simply brought more questions for Anna as she sat on the couch in the den flipping through channels just about as fast as she flipped through her thoughts.

She focused on them so she didn't have to think about spending another Christmas without family, without children running around, getting underfoot. Her children. She'd tried to fill that gap, that longing, by falling in love with the children of the orphanage. And it had definitely helped, but it wasn't the same.

So, she paid no heed to the signs of Christmas elegantly displayed before her, or just outside this room, the ivy entwining its way up the stair rail only to curl in and out of the banister overlooking the foyer. The smell of cinnamon and spice coming from the kitchen made her stomach growl, but she ignored it, still trying to think things through in a logical manner, shoving aside the emptiness Christmas always seemed to enhance.

While she was glad to see de Chastelain put away, the loose ends were definitely not tied up.

Who had been de Chastelain's help? He hadn't done all the dirty deeds himself, that was for sure. The incident with the helicopter on the ocean was proof of that. Sure, they'd arrested others in addition to de Chastelain, but had they arrested the *right* others?

Second, there was that missing body that she had seen but no one could ever even prove existed and seemed to have all but forgotten about. Was it really Brandon de Chastelain?

And third, who had pulled the trigger four years ago sending that bullet crashing into her? Who?

She was packed, ready to go. All set to get on the plane and head back to Brazil, to her children, her job as director. Yet, she hesitated. She couldn't let go of the feeling that there was something unfinished. Paulo would be fine. He grew stronger every day, no signs of infection or rejection having appeared.

"You ready for a little Christmas shopping?"

Anna looked up to see Lucas in the doorway, staring at her with a tender look in his eyes. Oh boy, better not investigate that one. Even if the look did make her feel all mushy inside. "I'm leaving, Lucas."

He froze, then carefully walked over to sit on the couch next to her.

"Why? I thought now that the danger was past and everything was settled…"

"But it's not settled. I've been over and over everything and it's not adding up."

He blew out an exasperated sigh. "I think you've been looking over your shoulder so long, you don't know how to stop. Could you just postpone leaving and give us chance?"

Biting back an acid retort, she stilled, thought about what he said, wondered if he could actually be right. Could she stop wondering if every person she ran into was after her? Could she slow down long enough to have a normal life? But he wanted children and she couldn't give him that. But still, what if…

Giving a small shrug, she looked him in the eye. "Maybe, maybe not."

He nudged her shoulder. "Maybe I'm right. So you want to go shopping?"

"What's this about shopping?" Thomas Bennett moved slowly over to the fireplace mantel to straighten an already straight candelabra.

"Hello, Father, I was just asking Anna if she'd like to do a little Christmas shopping."

"She's planning to stay for Christmas then?" He didn't sound as if he minded terribly.

Anna jumped in. "Ah, no sir, I probably won't be here. I really think I need to get back to the orphanage."

He turned, studied her, then gave a shrug. "Well, that's too bad. You actually liven the place up a bit."

Anna nearly giggled at the look on Lucas's face, then he gave a half smile and drawled, "Father, don't tell me you like Anna."

"Lucas, do grow up, won't you?"

Lucas shot her an amused look out of the corner of his eye. Anna had to look away or dissolve into unseemly laughter. When she looked back, in the blink of an eye, sadness had replaced his merriment and she gulped, her own joy fading. *Oh Lord, now would be a really good time to tell me what You want me to do.*

Lucas was just about to ask her to join him in a walk outside so they could talk privately when the front door opened, then banged shut a moment later. "Uncle Thomas?"

Godfrey was home.

"In here, boy."

Lucas's cousin stepped into the room pulling his leather gloves from his fingers. When he saw Lucas and Anna, he stopped, his smile faltering. "Oh, I didn't realize you were here." He looked back at his uncle. "I just needed you to sign some papers from the bank, but it can wait."

Standing, Lucas said, "Anna and I were just going Christmas shopping. I'll leave you to talk to Father."

"Nonsense, son," Thomas stepped forward and patted Lucas's shoulder as he looked over at Godfrey. "Now that Lucas is home, he'll want to be involved in everything businesswise. Now what are these papers?"

Godfrey cleared his throat. "Just your signature needed saying that you authorize that transfer of stock we talked about last week."

"Ah yes." He glanced at Lucas. "Giving some stock away to some charity deal that hit me up a couple of weeks ago. Might as well since it's getting close to the end of the year and the tax write-off will be nice." Thomas slipped his glasses on and peered at the papers, intently studied them, then said, "Mm-hmm. Looks good." With a flourish, he signed his name. Godfrey took the papers, set them on the coffee table in front of Anna and signed on the second line. Then he pulled out a second set and the two men went through the same routine. He then slipped them into the folder he held in his left hand.

Of course, there was always something in it for the old man. Shaking his head, Lucas watched the transaction then clapped Godfrey on the shoulder. "See you later, man." He glanced over at his father and whispered so only Godfrey could hear. "And God bless you." For dealing with my father. But he left that unsaid. The surprised laughter in Godfrey's eyes said he understood, though.

Anna had watched the entire exchange with a bemused expression on her face. Now, Lucas reached down, clasped her hand and pulled her to her feet. "I still want to go Christmas shopping."

"Funny," she said, tongue in cheek, "I don't remember you being that much of a shopper. If I recall correctly, you abhor shopping."

Refusing to believe she'd actually leave when all he wanted to do was wrap her in his arms and hold her close, he hid his feelings, determined to spend time with her and winked. "All depends on what you're shopping for."

Twenty minutes later, they walked into Valley View Mall. Christmas lights winked from every surface outside the mall, the charity bell-ringer stood at the entrance listlessly swinging his arm, his bored expression in direct contrast with the cheerful sound coming from his bell. Lucas dropped a twenty into the basket then reached over and took Anna's hand. She smiled up at him, yet the uncertain hesitation in her expression cut him. What held her back? De Chastelain was in jail, Justin had been cleared of any wrongdoing, so that had to make her feel a little better. True, there were still some unanswered questions, but those would be cleared up in time, right?

Anna glanced over her shoulder, her fingers warm yet tense in his grasp. Spying the store he wanted, he felt sweat break out over his forehead. *Um, God, I know I'm new to this praying thing, but if You could make this work out, I'd appreciate it.* Talking to God was becoming a habit. One that he was finding he liked—a lot. It made him feel…safe, comforted, and strong all at the same time. It was weird and if someone had tried to explain it to him, he would have thought they were crazy, but since it was something he felt, something he experienced, he couldn't deny it.

And now that he thought about it, Anna *had* tried to tell him. Wishing he'd listened a lot sooner, he smiled. It was good to be in love with a woman who was not only beautiful but smart, too.

"Lucas, where are you going?"

During his musings, his feet had brought him to the entrance to the store where his friend worked. Morrey's Jewelry.

Her eyes grew wide and she pulled her hand out of his. "I don't want to jump to conclusions or anything, but um…why are we coming here?"

Innocently, he reached into his pocket and pulled out a pair of breathtaking pearl earrings. "My father asked me to drop these off to have them cleaned. He said they were a present for someone for Christmas." He frowned. "Although I have to admit that it's odd. I have no idea who he's planning on giving them to. But I said I'd bring them. Is that all right?"

Red immediately suffused her cheeks and she nodded. "Sure, sure. Why don't you do that while I just kind of browse that rack of clothes over there?" She pointed to the clearance items displayed in front of a women's clothing store.

He flashed her a smile, hiding the hurt at her obvious reluctance to even enter the store with him, but he simply nodded and headed for the jewelry counter.

SIXTEEN

Anna felt sure her heart was going to pound right out of her chest. She'd thought…oh man, had she ever been more wrong in her life? She'd thought Lucas was going to take her in that store to look at rings.

Intense longing swept through her nearly doubling her over it was so strong. She wanted to look at rings with him, wanted that symbol of forever. Wanted that happily-ever-after promise. But she couldn't. She simply couldn't do that to him. He didn't know she couldn't have children and, while he'd not been overly vocal about it, she knew how important having his own children was to him.

His father certainly wanted grandchildren—and had the appropriate mother in mind. No doubt, those pearls were for Marybeth Ferris. And while the woman was right when she'd said that Lucas wanted reconciliation with his father, Anna didn't think he'd resort to marrying someone his father picked out for him. No, he'd almost made that mistake once. He wouldn't do that again.

"You ready?"

His warm breath tickled her ear and she shivered, swallowed hard and stepped away from him. Forcing a smile, she nodded. "Where to next?"

"Let's just walk. I want to show you something."

So they walked, her hand once again clasped in Lucas's strong one. From the corner of her eye, something flickered in one of the glass panes of the store window they just passed. She turned, looked, saw nothing. But that feeling of being watched was back and she shivered, the hair on the back of her neck standing straight up. Telling herself she was being ridiculous, she crossed her arms, rubbing them to get rid of the chill.

"Cold?"

"A little."

Wrapping his arm around her shoulder, he pulled her up close and they walked in step for a short distance. He stopped at an exit, pulled her through and let the door shut behind them.

Curious, she allowed him to lead her down the sidewalk and around the corner. A church stood in the distance, the steeple reaching for the white clouds floating gently overhead. He said nothing as he continued toward the church.

They crossed the parking lot and finally reached the front door of the building, only he didn't go in. Instead, he took the path around the side that led down a small hill to a prayer garden. Smiling at her, he said, "It's beautiful, isn't it? Even in December?"

Tall trees surrounded the area. Two benches sat strategically on either side of a man-made pond. A waterfall trickled over smooth stones, sounding soothing and peaceful, washing her stress away. "It's gorgeous, Lucas. I never knew this was here."

"My mother brought me here about a month before she died. I've never forgotten it. And I've never wanted to share it with anyone else. Until now." His heart shining from his sweeter than chocolate-brown eyes, Anna could only stare at the love she saw reflected there. She grew shaky, wondering where this was leading, yet fairly sure she knew. She searched her brain, tried to think of the right words to say, to tell him how much he meant to her but that she was all wrong for him.

"Lucas, I…"

He covered her lips with his thumb to quiet her then rubbed his thumb back and forth, causing her already trembling lips to tingle. "Don't say anything. It's taken me a long time to work up the nerve to do this."

"But don't say…"

Again, he stopped. "Shh. Let me do this, okay?"

She nodded, dreading what was coming, knowing it was time to tell him why she could never marry him and why he needed to find someone else.

He said, "I've watched you and cared about you for a long time. Now that this mess with someone trying to kill you is over, I think it's time to…tell you how I feel about you…and discuss the whole concept of God. I've definitely been thinking about Him and all that you've told me about Him. I've been praying." He sat down on the bench nearest to them, pulling her down next to him. The cold seeped through her jeans and she shivered again, shifting closer to his warmth even as she pondered the least painful way to push him away.

Taking her hand, he rubbed it between his palms and looked into her eyes. "I've made my peace with God, Anna. I went to church with my mother before she died. I've heard all about God, listened to the sermons in the little chapel in Brazil. I believe He's who you say He is. I didn't understand before, the relationship you have with Him, but as I've watched you and Paulo and re-membered things about Mark from college…I knew I was missing something. That day in the water, I honestly thought it was over for me—" he swallowed hard, looked away for a moment then back at her "—and I knew…I wasn't ready for death. I prayed and I believe God heard me. I can't explain how I know that, but I know He did." He quirked a smile.

"I know, Lucas, I can see the difference. Even if you'd never said anything to me, I would have known, just from watching you. I'm so glad." And she was. Thrilled for him, yet sad because she had to tell him that, while his decision was wonderful for him, it still didn't make a difference as far as a relationship between them went. And she had to be honest and tell him why.

"Anna, I want to…"

This time she was the one doing the silencing. She placed her fingers over his mouth and said, "Lucas, you want children and I—"

"Exactly," he broke in. "And I believe you'd be a great mother. You're the most wonderful, giving woman I know. You have all the qualities, the goodness…"

She stood, tears glistening on her lashes, shaking her head, backing away from him, her heart breaking. "I can't, Lucas. I can't have ch—"

The shot rang out, the bullet pinging off the bench where Lucas still perched. He rolled backward behind it and Anna dove down to join him.

Adrenaline surging, Lucas grabbed her hand, won-dering where the shot had come from. Anna, tense, jaw tight against her fear, gripped his fingers and gestured toward the church. Could they take cover there? Who was shooting? All the bad guys had been captured, right? His mind raced with the shock of knowing someone was still after Anna. Someone who'd slipped through the cracks.

Together, they raced for the cover of the church. What if it was locked? Another shot pinged off the door frame in front of them, causing them both to flinch and duck. Lucas sent up another prayer as they reached the door. The knob twisted and they rushed in to slam the door behind them.

Anna shook. Fear outlined her every feature, it came from her in waves. No doubt the sound of the gun had brought back every bad memory she had of the time she was shot. Bewilderment made her look like a child who'd had her trust completely shattered.

"Who?" she whispered.

Anger finally surfaced, shoving aside her fear. Fingers balled into fists, her breathing quickened. In the blink of an eye, she was in FBI mode, moving to the side window next to the door. She glanced out then moved to the next large window and looked out. Repeating this for the next four windows, she stopped at the one over-looking the parking lot.

"There! He's getting away."

Lucas rushed to her side to look over her shoulder. A dark gray sedan was pulling out of the lot at a fast clip. "Can you see the plate?"

"No. He's gone and your car is too far away to get to in time to chase him down."

He pulled her around to face him. "Anna, what's going on?"

Shaking her head, she stomped her foot in a fit of frustration. "I thought it was over. I thought…"

"What if we were wrong?" he asked. "What if it was never de Chastelain after you? What if the person who is trying to kill you is from another case? Do you have any more enemies out there who would come after you?"

A stunned look crossed her features. "I never considered…I have no idea, but I have to put an end to this. This time I'm leaving for good."

Pain speared him, so sharp, so cutting, it took his breath away. "Anna, I've already told you I'm in this with you to the end."

"This *is* the end, Lucas. I can't keep putting you in danger…and I can't be the mother of your children, I'm sorry. It's time for me to pack up and leave." And without a backward glance, she pulled the door open and walked out of the building. Tears in his eyes, he wondered if she was truly walking out of his life at the same time.

Raking a hand through his already mussed hair, he thought, fine, he'd let her have her space, let her leave. He'd go get himself together, visit Paulo, and then go back to his father's house to pack. He was going to go back to the only place he'd ever found any peace, any real meaning in his life. He was going back to Brazil.

Heart hurting, blood pounding, Anna stomped up the outside steps to Lucas's house, pulled open the front door and entered the foyer. With single-minded purpose, she made her way up the stairs to her room, mentally rehearsing her thank-you and her goodbye to Lucas's father and Godfrey. She'd tell Dahlia goodbye, too, if she ran into the woman. Other than that, she was out of here. De Chastelain was in jail, Justin was clean according to Jennifer, so there was no one else she could think of who would want her dead. Enough was enough. At the door of her room, she noticed nothing out of the ordinary. The door was still shut, just as she'd left it that morning. Twisting the knob, she pushed it open and stopped, glancing around. Everything was as it should be.

Breathing a sigh of relief, she began to grab her things and pack them in her usual orderly fashion thinking about her next step. What would she do? Where would she go? Lucas was done with her, had most likely given up on her. Not that she blamed him.

He'd probably go back to Brazil and while that had been Anna's original plan, she'd have to divert to Plan B. Because someone was still after her, and she couldn't lead a killer back to the children she loved.

Blowing out a sigh, she considered her options and came up with only one that somewhat satisfied her. She'd call Jennifer, ask if she could stay with her for a while, just until she figured something out. She'd have to let Jennifer know that her presence might possibly bring danger with it, but at least Jennifer was trained to deal with that kind of thing. Unlike Lucas.

Zipping the suitcase shut, she started packing her toiletries. Somewhere down the hall, a door slammed and she paused, fingering the shampoo bottle. Should she go ahead and say her goodbyes or keep packing?

Keep packing.

Tossing the remaining items into the small bag, she latched it and slung the handle over her wrist. Grabbing up her backpack, she reached down to snag the handle of the rolling suitcase. Fully loaded, she made her way out of the room and down the hall to the stairway.

"Oh, are you leaving?"

Dahlia walked to toward her, fiddling with a pin on her blouse.

Heaving an inward sigh, Anna forced a smile. "Yes, it's time for me to get going. Do you know if Ted's available to drive me?"

A shrug lifted the woman's thin shoulders. "Actually, no, he's not. He drove Thomas in for an appointment with his lawyer. However, I suppose you could take one of the cars from the garage and Ted could always pick it up later."

Relief allowed her to breathe a tad easier. "Wonderful." Hoisting her luggage, she made her way down the staircase, noticing Dahlia didn't bother to offer to help.

At the bottom, Anna set her bags on the floor. Maddy came in from the kitchen, purse slung over her shoulder, keys dangling in her hand. When she saw Anna was packed and ready to leave, her eyes went wide. "Oh, miss, I didn't know you were leaving."

Anna nodded and leaned over to give the woman a hug. "Yes, I guess so. I want to say thanks for everything. You've been awfully sweet."

Shrugging, Maddy said, "You're easy to be sweet to. Well, I'm off to pick up some groceries for dinner tonight." She leaned in for one more hug. "Please stay in touch."

"I will," Anna promised. Maddy rushed out the door and Dahlia swept past her amidst a cloud of recently applied perfume. Anna rubbed her nose and moved away slightly. She frowned. That scent bothered her. Not just because it was strong enough to knock her out but because it reminded her of…something. Brushing off the creepy sensation that she was missing something obvious, she started to ask Dahlia which car she should use when she noticed the pin Dahlia had been messing with earlier. Again, something stirred in the recesses of her memory. What was it about that perfume? She'd smelled it every day since she'd been here. What was her mind trying to tell her?

Her cell phone vibrated, cutting off her concentration. Answering it, she shifted to lean against the wall, her eye on the clock. "Hello?"

"Hey, it's Jennifer. I've got the name of the company that chopper belongs to. Exports Incorporated."

"Never heard of it."

"It recently changed its name from Bennett Incorporated."

She gasped. "Bennett Incorporated. That's Lucas's father's company."

"Really? Well, he's not listed as CEO. In fact I'm having trouble finding that person's name."

"Keep looking, will you? Something's weird about all this."

"You got it."

Anna hung up and frowned. On second thought, she did know that name. Exports Incorporated. She'd seen it on the papers Godfrey had brought for his father to sign earlier.

She sucked in a breath. Did Lucas's father hate her that much? Was he that determined to run Lucas's life that he would get rid of the "unsuitable" woman he thought Lucas might marry by killing her off? At the risk of killing his son in the process? But that made no sense. Lucas's father hadn't even know she existed until she met him that day someone almost ran them off the road. She slapped a hand to her forehead. She'd wind up with a serious headache if she kept this up. One way or another she was going to find out what was going on. But she had to do it from somewhere other than Lucas's home. If something happened to him because of her, she'd never forgive herself.

Lucas flipped his cell phone shut. He'd checked in with Mark to see how Paulo was doing. The little guy was continuing to recover nicely. However, his buddy and roommate, Andy, wasn't doing so well and Paulo kept asking when Andy was going to get his new heart. Unfortunately, neither Lucas nor Mark had a good answer for him.

Now, he had nothing else to think about, to distract his mind from thoughts of Anna. Lucas slammed his fist against the steering wheel of his car. Sitting outside the popular little coffee shop, he pondered his heart. He was *not* going back to Brazil, at least not without Anna. He was going to find that stubborn woman and convince her to stop running. Or at least get her to change direction and run into his arms. A light tapping on his passenger-door window pulled him reluctantly from his planning.

Marybeth stood there, impatiently waiting for him to roll down his window. What did she want?

His finger snagged the window control and the glass slid smoothly down. Marybeth leaned in and gave him a sweet smile. He had to admit she was very beautiful. But her beauty didn't move him. Admiring her was like admiring a beautiful piece of artwork or a painting, one that showed promise but not much warmth or emotion. Still, he let her open the passenger door and slide into the seat beside him.

"Hello, Lucas. All alone this afternoon?"

"What do you want, Marybeth?" He didn't have the time or the inclination to deal with this woman. Not when he had Anna on his mind and in his heart.

His curt tone seemed to set her back a moment, and a flash of anger appeared in her sapphire eyes. But she recovered quickly and leaned closer. He pulled back and eyed her warily. Taking the hint, she put some space between them, looked down at her hands folded in her lap. "I miss Lance, Lucas."

She may have put some physical space between them, but her words quickly had him feeling trapped... and a little sorry for her. "I know you do, Marybeth, but it's been three years. You've got to let him go."

Sadness briefly flickered before she glanced away. "I've loved him since I was five and we had our pretend wedding down by the dock. I don't know how to let him go."

He wanted to say, *Stop hanging around my family, move on and get a life.* Instead, he settled for some gentle honesty. "I can't replace him, you know. No matter what you and my father have schemed up. I don't love you."

Vulnerability shone through and he realized Marybeth had a whole other side to her personality that she didn't let anyone else see. Quickly, she masked it and said coolly, "You haven't tried to love me, Lucas. In fact, every time I come around you, you act like I'm contagious."

He owed her an apology as he certainly hadn't meant to make her feel like that. It's just his father and his manipulations made him so antsy. He blew out a sigh. "Marybeth, I'm sorry. I never meant..."

She cut him off. "You're in love with *her,* aren't you?"

Not bothering to deny it, he just looked at her. Her features hardened before him, changing her, making her look ugly, worn and old. She sneered, "Why would you love a little nobody, someone who comes from nothing and isn't worth the dust you shake from your shoes?" Lucas felt the anger snake through him, but he bit his tongue, reminding himself to tread carefully. She was hurting, had been hurting for a long time. But her next words left him speechless.

"She's a barren, homeless nobody who'll never give you the one thing I can. Your own biological children. That's right, Lucas, she can't have children. She had a hysterectomy four years ago when she was shot."

SEVENTEEN

She just couldn't put her finger on what she was missing, so she'd not think about it and maybe her subconscious would come up with an answer. "Could I get a set of keys from you before you go?" What the woman did all day long, Anna had yet to figure out, but right now that was the least of her concerns.

"Of course."

Dahlia walked into the kitchen then came back and handed her the keys. "Just take the silver Jag. I'm going to go sit in the garden for a while."

Anna thanked her and grabbed up her things to cart them to the garage. Dahlia wandered off to do whatever Dahlia did and Anna forced herself not to think about leaving. *God, I really don't want to leave, I want to marry Lucas and have his children and it hurts that I can't. Really, really hurts.*

Shoving the aching emptiness aside, she opened the kitchen door to pass through the sunroom and on into the attached multicar garage. Setting her large suitcase on the floor, she decided to pull the car out first in order to avoid dinging any doors while she loaded up.

The sunroom door led to the garage. She knew this

simply from the architectural structure, but had never been in this part of the house, had no reason to come out here.

Exports Incorporated. That name had been in big bold letters at the top of the first paper Thomas Bennett had signed. Chewing her lip, she decided to put her things in the car, then call Lucas and ask him about it. She hoped he would answer his phone when his caller ID flashed her number.

Her phone rang once more. Jennifer again.

She flipped it open. "What do you have?"

"The CEO of Exports Incorporated is listed as Godfrey Bennett. But get this. The name changed only two months ago. The same time Godfrey took over as CEO."

"Godfrey! That doesn't make any sense. Why would he want to kill me?"

Three steps led down to where the cars were kept. The closest car was the silver Jaguar and it gleamed in the overhead light. The second space stood empty, probably where the Roadster shut down at night. The third space held the Mercedes.

A black Mercedes. "Hey Jennifer, I'll call you back later, okay?" She clicked the phone closed.

Suspicion darkening her thoughts, she scooted around the Jag and made her way over to the big black car. The front grille gleamed, not a scratch on it. Still, she walked around to the back. The license plate read DAHLIA1.

A glimmer of awareness tickled her mind.

It had been Lucas's car that had been tampered with.

Lucas's boat that had been targeted.

The bullet in the prayer garden had pinged the bench—next to Lucas.

And she knew.

Nobody was after her.

Somebody was after Lucas. But who was the guy in the hospital who'd warned her away? And why?

"Well, I guess I'm going to have to get rid of you the hard way." Anna spun to face the man who'd uttered those mild-sounding, terror-inducing words. A single flick of his wrist had the door to the garage coming down. Anna dashed to make it under the door before it closed. "Stop now or I'll shoot."

Small but deadly, the barrel of the pistol zeroed in on her like a homing device.

Backpedaling, fear causing her to tremble, to be clumsy, she whirled around and stumbled against the golf bag, knocking it over, sending the balls and clubs rolling from their holding place.

She ignored them, her only thought to get away from the gun. Get away, get away. Get to the help that glowed from the number pad near the door. If she could punch in the right code, she could have the police on the way. But first, she had to get to it and *he* was in the way. Could she draw him out, away from the door? She ducked back behind the Mercedes, hovering there, garage wall to her back. "Godfrey, what are you doing?"

Hating the wobble in her voice, she forced it aside. *You're an FBI agent, now's a good time to act like it.* Ignoring the memories of the feel of a bullet tearing into her abdomen, she sent up prayers for wisdom and a hedge of protection. Just as she was about to move, a voice from the door asked, "Godfrey, why do you have that gun?"

"Dahlia, go back inside. I'm thinking about selling it and checking to make sure I have all the parts," he ordered, without taking his eyes from Anna, who was hidden from Dahlia's view. She shivered at his cold, exact words. Anna wanted to scream at the woman to call the cops, but the look on Godfrey's face told her if she said a word, he wouldn't hesitate to pull the trigger—and kill both of them. Her fear tripled as Dahlia obeyed her husband and meekly slipped back inside, never knowing Anna's life hung in the balance.

"Ok, Godfrey, I guess it's just us." Desperately, she tried to buy some time. Her location didn't offer Godfrey a very good shot, but if she moved, she'd be out in the open. She shifted and her foot kicked one of the golf clubs. Could she...

"Yes, I guess it is."

"You were never after me, were you?"

He smirked. "No, you were just pretty much in the wrong places at the wrong times. Collateral damage and all that rot. I did try to warn you away, but apparently Silas isn't as scary as he used to be."

"The man who tried to kill me in the hospital."

"Hmm. Comes from a long line of killers, but you just wouldn't leave, were constantly with Lucas. I never could get him alone to get rid of him. And I certainly couldn't do anything here at the house that would throw suspicion back on me." He looked around. "Unfortunately, you've left me with no choice."

Anna sucked in a deep breath, desperate to buy some time. "What about Lucas?" she blurted. "Why not have Silas just kill him?"

A cold laugh escaped Godfrey. "Because Lucas was *mine.*"

"So you're responsible for all the other attacks."

"Indeed. Now shut up and get in the car. I can't shoot you here."

Her mind whirling, she moved her foot an inch to settle on the widest part of the club that was used to hit the ball. Somehow she had to figure out a way to use it as a weapon. Godfrey shifted away from the door trying to get a better bead on her. She moved in sync, snapping the golf club handle up into her hand.

A small measure of relief flowed through her. She wasn't completely helpless. Keep him talking. Keep him off guard. Buy time to think, plan, get away. "What did Lucas ever do to you?"

"He came back."

Holding the club against her leg, to her side, she waited. Godfrey moved again to the left, so she moved to the left. "And that's a problem because…?"

"Because he'll reconcile with his father and I'll be written out of the will. What do you think the old man's appointment was about this morning? He was going to put Lucas back in his will. I don't understand how one man could be so hard to kill." She could almost hear his teeth grinding, but the blank expression on his face never faltered.

"Why not just kill Thomas while you were in the will? Why go after Lucas?" Anna said. He shifted once more, Anna two-stepped with him, keeping the car in between them. He came closer, but at least he kept talking.

"I can't get rid of the old man yet. I still need his signatures on certain papers."

"What for?"

"For the share of the business to be transferred into my name. Everything to be transferred into my name. My new business, Exports Incorporated. One that Lucas'll never be able to get his hands on. Everything is almost finished."

Anna moved again. He was getting too close.

The gun raised, pointed in her direction. She ducked and blurted, "Why not just forge his signature?"

"No, I need his authentic one. An expert could tell the difference and then everything would be lost."

"But why would he sign papers without reading them?"

"Because he can't read well anymore. Not since the stroke. His pride suffered a severe blow, but he needed help to hide this shortcoming from his board and others." A smug chuckle escaped the man. "And dear old Godfrey was here to pick up the pieces. Fortunately, he trusts me. I just tell him what's in there and he signs them."

Feeling sad for the man who'd been betrayed and taken advantage of by his own flesh and blood, Anna concentrated on the gun. "And you think Lucas would interfere in the business if he decided to stay? To move home permanently?"

"Of course. It would be only a matter of time before he figured everything out and felt obligated to do whatever he could to help the father he wants to reconcile with."

"He's a doctor. He has no interest in the family business."

Godfrey guffawed. "If he moved home, Uncle Thomas would give Lucas no choice in the matter. No, it's best if he just ceases to exist. If he'd stayed in Brazil, none of this would be an issue. All my life, I watched Lance and Lucas live like kings. Now it's my turn. I'm almost there. Officially, I am now the owner of just about everything. A few more signatures and I will be the one sitting pretty. There's no way I'm going to let you and Lucas ruin what I've planned for over three years."

"Three years? But Thomas only had the stroke a year…" Horrified, she realized what he'd said without saying it. She whispered, "You blew up the boathouse, didn't you?"

Shock zipped through his eyes for a brief moment, shock that she'd figured it out. Then he shrugged. "Lucas was supposed to die in that, too, but he left before the timer ran out."

Lucas stepped into the foyer and shut the door behind him, bent on finding Anna and talking some sense into her. Was she even still here? Had Ted taken her to wherever she'd planned to go? Was he too late? And what was Godfrey's car doing in the driveway?

"Father? Maddy? Godfrey?" Silence.

He stepped into the kitchen and stopped short. His father stood beside the intercom. At least he thought it was his father. The pale, suddenly fragile looking man who was sweating profusely looked old. Nothing like his father.

"Father?"

The man started, looked up at Lucas with a terrible hurt in his now rheumy eyes. Lucas noticed the details of his father's breathing, short gasps as if he wasn't getting enough air, the blue tinge to his lips, right hand rubbing his left arm.

He was having a heart attack. Lucas immediately went into doctor mode, his mind racing with what he needed to do to keep his father alive.

Crossing the room, he touched his father's shoulder. "Come on, Dad, I need you to lie down, right here for a minute. Just to catch your breath. You'll feel better in a minute if you rest."

"Anna…"

"Shh. Don't say anything. I'm going to call for some help."

"Called cops." More wheezing gasps.

Just as Lucas grabbed his father under his arms, the man's legs gave out. Gently lowering him to the floor, he reached behind him to grasp a chair and pull it over. Picking his father's legs up, he placed them on the chair to keep the blood and oxygen flowing to the major organs. Getting up, he rummaged through the medicine cabinet until he found some aspirin. Placing one of the dissolvable tablets under his father's tongue, he asked, "Why did you call the cops? You need the paramedics."

"Anna…in danger…garage."

Lucas stilled. "Anna's in danger?"

"Intercom."

He glanced up at the device on the wall. Someone had left it on. Most likely his father when he'd called for Ted to take him to his appointment this morning. He reached up to shut it off and froze when he heard Godfrey's voice. "Lucas was supposed to die in that, too, but he left before the timer ran out."

"Why don't you put the gun down? You won't get away with this." Anna.

"Oh how cliché. Of course I'll get away with it. Who's going to stop me?"

Torn between staying with his father and rushing to Anna's aid, he hesitated, praying for the paramedics and the cops to get here. Anna was holding her own with Godfrey in the garage, but he wasn't sure how much longer she had before Godfrey got tired of talking and started shooting. Godfrey! What was going on?

Keeping an ear peeled for the police, he loosened his

father's collar, got a cool cloth and placed it on his forehead. Taking his father's wrist, he felt for the pulse. It was weak, thready and he was running out of time. He had to get to Anna, but he couldn't let his father die.

Anna crouched, golf club gripped tight. Godfrey was insane. Certifiable. He honestly believed he was going to be able to shoot her and get away with it. Sweat beaded her forehead and her breaths came in shallow pants.

"Come on, Anna, just make this easy and it'll all be over fast. I won't make you suffer, I promise. But I can't let you go. You'd just warn Lucas."

Exactly why she had to stay alive. To warn Lucas. Silent, she moved again, her ears straining to hear his every move, trying to anticipate which way he'd go. She was almost all the way around the Mercedes, her back to the electric garage door, the door to the sunroom and kitchen were to her left. Godfrey should be in front of the silver Jag according to the sounds of his shuffling. Did she dare dart out to try and get to the opposite side of the Jag? No, that would be suicide, leaving her exposed long enough for him to plant a bullet in her.

He crept closer, closing in on her. Only this time she waited. She had to get out of this herself. No one knew she was here. *Please God, show me what to do.*

Pulse pounding, she forced herself to wait. To be patient, regulate her breathing. One more step. Godfrey kicked a stray golf ball, the clatter of which almost startled her into a scream. She choked it back.

"Come on Anna, where are you?"

Hoping the tire hid her feet should he look under the car, she waited. Labeled boxes, still unpacked almost a year after Godfrey's and Dahlia's move, lined the wall. Some were stacked as tall as she was, and provided some shelter from his view. He couldn't look around them, nor under them.

Cautious, she felt him coming, the hairs on her neck standing up in warning.

Then she bolted. A shot rang out, pinged off the top of the Jaguar and hit the wall above her head. She slammed the garage door opener with her palm, then ducked back down. The door slid open to the sound of Godfrey's curses. She couldn't get out yet, she'd be too exposed. But maybe with the door open he'd lose a little of that iron control and extreme confidence.

With the end of the golf club, not raising her head, she used the rubber handle to punch in the code to bring the police. Another shot sounded and hit the code box.

Had she pushed the buttons in time? Pulling the golf club back down to her, she heard Godfrey rounding the car. This time instead of running she surprised him, met him face-to-face, looked into his mad, empty eyes, then swung the club as hard as she could. It caught his hand. "Ah!"

The weapon tumbled from his suddenly numb fingers, which is what she'd hoped would happen. The gun skittered under the Mercedes. She swung the club again, catching him in the knee. He went down.

Groaned.

Then looked up. Grabbed the gun from underneath the car.

And lunged.

Lucas heard the gunshot and flinched. His father's breathing had grown shallower, his pulse weaker. The paramedics rushed in the door and Lucas said, "Heart attack. Give him some nitro and oxygen and airlift him to the hospital. I'll meet you there." Lucas raced through the sunroom to the garage, knowing Godfrey had probably heard the ambulance sirens and was going to be desperate to get rid of Anna before being discovered.

Throwing open the garage door, he saw Godfrey going after Anna. "Godfrey!"

Godfrey swung around, raised the gun and fired. His aim was off, the bullet went wide. Lucas kept after him, hoping to keep his attention focused away from Anna, giving her time to flee. Godfrey, realizing what was happening, uttered a curse, fired off another round that came close enough to make Lucas flinch and hit the ground. Godfrey turned and went after Anna.

His heart racing, and breath coming in panicked gasps, Lucas scrambled to his feet and sped after the two of them, catching up close enough to see Anna duck into the boathouse.

Godfrey was nowhere in sight. Where had the man gone? Cold fear settled in his stomach. It was one thing to have your enemy in plain sight, it was another to know he was there, but be unable to pinpoint his location.

Expecting a bullet to come out of nowhere, Lucas ducked behind a tree to catch his breath and scan the area. Normally the rolling lawn held green, sodded grass. Right now, it was a plain, crisp brown revealing no sign of Godfrey. Where could he be?

The cement driveway led to the boathouse. And Anna.

He had to get to her.

His eyes pierced the area around him, and saw

nothing, heard nothing. Lucas took off toward the building that held Anna…and a lot of bad memories, praying the police would arrive soon.

Godfrey had to be right behind her. Panting, fear pushing her adrenaline to new levels, she desperately searched for a way out. Daylight streamed through the windows, but other than that it was dark. However, hiding would just delay the inevitable. The boathouse was big, but not big enough to dodge bullets.

Could she get in a boat, head out to sea? But that would mean leaving Lucas in danger. Huh, nope. Okay, so that wasn't an option.

The door slammed. She whirled, dove behind a speedboat.

She'd dropped the golf club so she needed to find a weapon. Her eyes darted here. There. Nothing.

"Anna." The sing-songy voice came from behind her.

The back door. He'd come in the back door.

She stilled, willing her heart to stop racing, her breathing to slow. Control. Then she started playing the game once again. She moved as silently as possible, sliding her hand along the boat's exterior, moving, stopping to listen. Hearing nothing.

Where was he? He'd been there to her right just moments ago.

A shuffle, a shaft of light across her face. Slinking back away, she tried to melt into the shadows.

"Come on, Anna. Lucas knows you're in here. He's on his way. He doesn't know about me, though. He thinks he lost me, that I ran away." She shuddered at the casual conversation tone. He was nuts.

Another scuff to her left. Her legs cramped from her crouched position, muscles burning, the smell of gasoline and oil making her nose burn. *Please, Jesus, help…when I am afraid, when I am afraid, when I am afraid…*

"Anna." He reverted to the singsong voice that stirred the nausea in her gut. "Come out, come out wherever you are. Because if you don't, as soon as Lucas comes through that door looking for you, I'm going to shoot him."

Shifting to her right, her fingers brushed wood. A stick? With her palm, she felt the shape of it. Smooth and flat on top, rounding at the edge. A paddle.

Better yet…a weapon. *I will trust in You.*

Lucas twisted the knob to the building that he'd had to work up the courage to enter when he'd first returned from Brazil. He'd hated the bad memories, memories he couldn't shake thousands of miles away, but with Anna's help and presence, he'd been able to let the good memories overshadow the bad. And now Godfrey was threatening everything Lucas held dear.

At least he thought so. He hadn't actually seen Godfrey go into the boathouse, but that didn't mean he hadn't used the other door. Had the man realized it was hopeless and run?

And where were the cops? He should be hearing sirens by now.

Caution dictating every movement, he pulled the door open and slipped inside. He moved to the right, next to the now shut door and stood there a moment letting his eyes adjust to the dimness.

A clicking sound to his left caught his attention, then

he felt the impact of a body slamming into his, knocking him to the floor. The bullet hit the wall where he'd been standing, sending wood chips raining down on him. He breath gone, his entire being stunned, he pushed all that aside and reacted.

Something brushed by him. He grabbed, caught a wrist...and paused.

"It's me," Anna whispered. "We need to move."

"Great, Anna, you really messed up a good shot. All of this would almost be over if you'd have just kept still." Godfrey sounded bored.

Lucas pulled Anna with him as he scrabbled behind a five-foot-tall tool chest. Panting, she sat beside him and pulled something into her lap.

Another crack sounded at the same time a brief flash of light stuttered the darkness. This time, the object that hit him pierced the flesh of his right arm spinning him around and back to the floor of the boathouse. Pain sent him reeling. He'd been shot. Stunned, he lay there for a moment, then realized the bullet had passed through the muscle of his bicep. Painful but not fatal.

Anna screamed, leaped to her feet, raised the wooden weapon and swung it like a baseball bat. Godfrey hollered, but grabbed the paddle and grappled with her, knocking her back down and landing on top of her.

Twisting, she fought him, but then he brought the gun around to her face and she faltered. Lucas could almost see the rush of memories from when she'd been shot before, but he hesitated, reining in the almost over-powering desire to tackle Godfrey, not wanting to make the wrong move that got her shot.

Using a self-defense move she'd probably learned in

FBI training, she brought her hand up sideways to smash it against her assailant's arm. Godfrey yelped, but held on to the weapon. Using the heel of her hand, she brought it up to meet his nose with enough force to break it. Blood spurted and Godfrey screamed his pain and rage as he arched back in agony. Lucas dove on top of him, scraping his elbow against the concrete, his bullet wound throbbing unmercifully as he grasped the hand still clutching the gun. Godfrey struggled, the weapon waving wildly, but Lucas was stronger and he held on, squeezing as hard as he could.

It was only then he registered he'd heard the sirens, now silent. A door slammed open, rushing feet arrived on the scene. Gun drawn, one tall, well-built officer yelled, "Freeze! Drop the gun!"

Lucas's first instinct was to do as ordered and freeze, but that would mean letting Godfrey get a free hand out to slug him—or shoot him. So, Lucas held on, struggling to get the gun away from Godfrey's adrenaline-induced strength.

"Godfrey! Stop!" Dahlia's screech startled her husband into a pertinent pause, giving Lucas the opening he needed. Jerking his knee up into his cousin's stomach, the breath whooshed from the man's lips and his grip weakened enough for Lucas to pull the weapon out of his hand.

And still, the man didn't stop until Anna retrieved the paddle she'd dropped and swung it into his stomach. While he was bent double one officer reached down and pushed Godfrey the rest of the way to the ground then shoved a knee in his back.

Godfrey hollered and finally quit struggling, blood dripping from his broken nose. Once he had the cuffs on him, the officer pulled Godfrey to his feet, another helped Lucas up.

Anna stood in the dim light, a stunned look on her face, the paddle still clutched in her fist. Ignoring his wounded arm, Lucas rushed over to her to grab a hand and pull her to him and she fell, almost limp against his chest. Their harsh goodbyes forgotten, he clasped her to him and held her, relishing the feel of her safe in his arms.

Once Godfrey had been arrested and information about the man named Silas was passed on to the authorities, Lucas made Anna promise to stick around so they could talk after all the madness died down. She'd agreed and was now inside the house taking a quick shower to rinse the blood off and change into clean clothes.

Dahlia had gone along with Godfrey's loud protestations declaring he didn't mean it—he was just trying to take care of her. Investigators had already been assigned to look into Godfrey's business dealings and the helicopter pieces they'd fished out of the water had been matched with that of the logo of Dahlia's cosmetics business. Godfrey had been using her business to funnel funds into it, stashing away megabucks, stealing his uncle blind.

Before the police hauled Godfrey off, Lucas had looked at him, not bothering to hide the hurt, the betrayal he felt at his cousin's actions. "Why?"

Godfrey had smirked, shaken his head and said, "Because I could. You've always had everything. My father struggled, scraped to get by and Uncle Thomas refused to do anything to help him. My mother worked herself into an early grave and I watched it all. You and Lance, everything you touched turned to gold. Then I managed to get Lance hooked on drugs and he hooked me on money, lots of it. I decided to get my hands on as much of it as possible and when Uncle Thomas had his stroke and asked me to help take care of the business, it was the perfect opportunity." He snarled. "Then you had to come home and ruin it."

Feeling ill at the memory of that confrontation and the hate in the eyes of the cousin he'd loved like a brother, Lucas stepped into his father's house, the scrape on his arm throbbing, the bullet wound adding to his assortment of bruises. He ignored it, knowing it was minor and that he could get it taken care of shortly. He'd have to have it cleaned out and take some antibiotics, but he'd be fine. The police had their required report, so all was well on that end.

His father was the one who's health was in question and Lucas was ready to get to the man's side.

As soon as Anna was finished cleaning up from her encounter with Godfrey's broken, bloody nose, they'd head to the hospital. Mark was already there, promising to take care of the old man and do his best to keep the damage to the man's heart to a minimum. Thomas was still alive, hanging on. Mark assured Lucas he could take his time getting to the hospital as his father would be going through test after test. He would be admitted to ICU until he was stabilized.

Two minutes later, Anna came down the steps, hair still wet, her eyes not meeting his.

He said, "We'll talk after we find out about my father, if that's all right."

Softening, she said, "Of course. Let's go."

* * *

Two hours later, Lucas stepped into his father's room. Machines beeped and whirred. The oxygen mask over the man's face made him look even more fragile than he had lying on the kitchen floor. Color had returned to his face, but he wasn't totally out of the woods yet.

The door opened behind him and he turned to see Mark enter. "Hey."

Lucas shook his head. "I can't believe that's my dad lying there. I've never seen him so…helpless."

Mark's hand came down on his shoulder in a gesture of comfort. "He's stable. Barely. We need to keep a close eye on him, but at least he's responding to the drugs and seems to be breathing a lot better."

"This was all a terrible shock for him." Lucas filled his friend in on everything that had occurred. Mark gave a low whistle.

"Yeah, pretty crazy, huh? So, when is he going to wake up?"

Shrugging, Mark moved in to adjust the buttons on one of the machines. "I don't know. I kind of thought he might stir a little before now."

"Anna will be up in a minute. She went to check on Paulo. I think she just wanted to give me some time with my father."

"That's a classy lady you've got there."

"Don't I know it. Only I don't have her yet." He blew out a sigh, thinking of all the talking they still had to do.

Mark clapped him on the back again. "You will."

Lucas certainly hoped so but wasn't quite as confidant as his buddy. Mark left and he turned to find his father's eyes trained on him. Taking the man's gnarled, spotted hand in his, he stared back into the face that had never once said, "I love you" to his son. He gazed down at the man who didn't seem to have a compassionate bone in his body or understand the word mercy. And in that moment, Lucas made a decision. He said, "I love you, Dad."

At first he wondered if his father heard him. Then one tear made a silent trek down the side of his father's face, crossed his temple and disappeared into the shell of his ear. A feeble squeeze tightened his fingers, bringing a lump to Lucas's throat. Was that all it took? Just saying those three little words?

Thomas's hand came up, fumbled with the oxygen mask then managed to pull it off. "I'm sorry, Lucas. For everything…don't blame you for Lance's death," he wheezed.

"Shh, don't talk, Dad, it's okay."

"I…admire you. You followed…your dream."

Swallowing hard, Lucas wondered if he'd heard the man right. "Thanks, Dad. Now, be quiet and get some rest. If you have a relapse, Mark'll kill me."

The ghost of a smile crossed the old man's lips. "I…always wanted to be a…doctor. You did it. Good for you. Proud of you." He let the oxygen mask slip back on, then his eyes shut and a measure of peace seemed to come over his features. In shock, unable to find any more words in his suddenly scrambled brain, thanks to his father's confession, Lucas figured everything else he had to say could wait.

Now, he had to find Anna. She was probably with Paulo. He'd check there first.

Making her way to Paulo's room, Anna dreaded the upcoming talk with Lucas, but it was time. She understood that he wasn't ready to leave the hospital because of his father, so they'd find someplace private when he was free. She knew he was in love with her and possibly even wanted to tell her so. And she needed to come clean about why she couldn't marry him.

She couldn't just leave without being honest. That wasn't fair. It was time to face one of her biggest fears. Telling the man she loved she could never have his child. Getting shot at almost didn't compare to the fear now filling her. She choked back the sobs that threatened, fiercely telling herself she had to get through this. She'd survive. *Please let me do this without falling apart, God.*

She made her way up to Paulo's room and Anna found Lucas already there. He turned to smile but she saw the seriousness in Lucas's eyes and wondered what he was thinking.

"Will you go to church with me Christmas Eve?" he asked.

That wasn't the question she thought he'd been going to ask. But… "Sure, I'd love to. Then I guess I need to start thinking about the future and what I'm going to do with it."

Lucas merely smiled and put an arm around her shoulders. "Well, I can promise you this. You're not doing it without me."

"Or me," Paulo piped up.

EIGHTEEN

Christmas Eve blew in with a flurry of freezing temperatures and good cheer. Anna walked up the steps to the church breathing in the scent of firewood and spiced cider, cinnamon punch and just…Christmas. It smelled like Christmas. The stars twinkled on a canopy of black as she waited for Lucas to catch up with her. They'd spent a lot of the day at the hospital just visiting and talking with Lucas's father and entertaining Paulo. And she'd never gotten around to telling him she couldn't have children. But she didn't want to ruin his Christmas, either.

Anna had asked Lucas to go to the Christmas Eve service with her at Ted and Joni's church. He'd agreed and her heart felt full. He'd parked the car and was now jogging across the lot. Finally, he stepped up beside her, grinned down at her and took her hand.

She grinned back. "Ready?"

"With you by my side, I'm ready for anything."

"You're so corny, you know that?" The twinkle in her eye probably exposed the fact she was teasing, but that was okay.

Laughter rumbled from him and he swept her up in a bear hug. "Lucas, put me down!"

"Oh, Edith, would you look at that." The warbled voice reached Anna and she flushed with embarrassment as a little old lady with gray hair and her companion walked past her and into the church. The lady who must be Edith turned back and gave her a wink.

Lucas gave another deep chuckle that tickled her ear. "Corny or not, I mean it."

What a scene they were making right there on the church steps. She'd never seen Lucas so…so…so… free, unaffected and unburdened. It made her heart sing. Not that he was over what had happened with his family; of course that would take time. But as soon as he realized he was in no way responsible for his brother's death, a weight seemed to lift from his shoulders. He still grieved Lance's death, but in a new way. It was grief free of guilt. He was working on the anger he felt toward Godfrey, but had already told Anna there was no way he was letting that ruin the rest of his life.

They walked on into the church and snagged a pew halfway down the aisle. The aisle she envisioned walking down one day with Lucas waiting for her on the other end. The vision sent shivers all through her. Good shivers. Scary shivers. They still had one more issue to discuss and she dreaded it. Refusing to let that cast a pall over her day, she shrugged out of her coat and gloves, placing them on the pew beside her in anticipation of the worship experience to come. Strains from the piano played softly as the pews filled. Hushed pre-service chattering went on around her and she smiled as Joni slipped in to sit beside her. Ted shook hands with Lucas, who then wrapped an arm around Anna's shoulders and snuggled her tight up under his arm. Spicy cologne tickled her nose and she knew it would be a scent she'd never be able to smell without thinking of him.

Thank you, Lord.

Peace filled her. It would be all right. The Lord would work it out. Somehow.

The service started and the Christmas music she loved so much filled the air. The pastor read the Christmas story from Luke 2 while Anna smiled and thought of Paulo. She'd be sure to read it to him tomorrow.

On the way out of the church, Anna's cell phone vibrated in her pocket. Looking at the number, she frowned.

"Who is it?" Lucas asked, noting her troubled expression.

"Justin. What does he want?"

"Are you going to answer it?"

Sighing, she flipped it to her ear and said, "Hello, Justin."

"Merry Christmas, Anna."

"You should be home with your family. What are doing working?"

"You know the bad guys never take time off."

Unfortunately, she knew that only too well. "So what do you have?"

"Your boyfriend's hunch was right. The dead body was de Chastelain's twin."

Taking a deep breath, she said flatly, "You found him."

"De Chastelain talked, big time. He's trying to go for a reduced sentence. Apparently, after all those years, Brandon showed up at an inopportune moment to pay brother Shawn a visit. When Brandon realized what was going on, he threatened to turn Shawn in. Unable to let that happen, Shawn killed him."

"But the camera in the room was turned off."

"Simple, remote control. Wouldn't take two seconds."

"What else?" She glanced at Lucas, who was helping one of the elderly women down the steps of the church. The little lady smiled up at him, patted his hand, then whispered something in his ear. Lucas grinned and nodded.

Anna focused back on what Justin was saying. "We also know who shot you that day."

Okay, now her knees felt a little weak. "Who?" she breathed.

"De Chastelain's wife."

"What?" She didn't like the squeaky sound of her voice but couldn't seem to help it.

"When we found the brother's body, buried under a storage shed out back, we found gloves and the same black mask that we caught on the surveillance videos. Our forensics people pulled some hair from the mask and were able to match up the DNA with de Chastelain's wife."

"But…why?"

"Apparently, de Chastelain was obsessed with finding you and killing you. It was all he could focus on."

"And Sherry's jealousy finally got the better of her," Anna surmised. "I bet she hung out around that office daily. Just waiting for the perfect moment. The protest demonstration provided her a great opportunity. Cover, confusion, diverted focus. Yes, indeed, she couldn't pass that up, could she? I bet she saw the news coverage on TV and hauled herself over there." Anna blew out a sigh. "All the loose ends are nicely wrapped up now, right?"

"Looks like it. I just wanted to call and let you know. Enjoy your Christmas."

"Hey, Justin?"

"Yeah?"

"I'm sorry I suspected you."

A pause. "I guess I can't blame you. Once Jennifer explained it, I would have thought you were crazy if you *hadn't* suspected me."

"But we've been friends forever and I owe you an apology."

"Like I said, don't sweat it. It all worked out in the end."

"Thanks, Justin. You have a merry Christmas, too."

"You gonna come back to work?"

Anna looked over at Lucas, standing next to the two little old women, making their day by flirting sweetly with both of them. "Naw, I've got a bigger and better job ahead of me."

"That Lucas fellow?"

"Yeah, that Lucas fellow and hopefully a little boy named Paulo." Maybe. Depending on how bad Lucas wanted biological children.

Christmas Day dawned bright and beautiful with not a snow cloud in sight. The snow machine spurted out flake after flake. Before going up to get Paulo, Lucas said he wanted Anna to see the sight. She gasped in awe. Man-made snow covered the large area of green grass outside the hospital right under Paulo's window. The wide expanse was about the size of a basketball court and was already about two feet deep.

Lucas turned to Anna. "Do you think we could have a talk?"

"I guess it's time, isn't it?"

He led her to a small bench resembling the one in the little prayer garden outside the hospital. The wind blew a chilly breeze, but it was the ice in her heart that chilled her from the inside out. So, this was it. She gave a nervous chuckle. "I hope this little visit doesn't end the same way as the one near the mall."

"Not a chance. All the bad guys are in jail." He reached over and took her hand. She flinched but didn't pull away. "I'm in love with you, Anna. I want to marry you."

"I can't have children," she blurted. There. She'd said it.

"I know." The calm acceptance in his eyes stilled her heart for a beat or two. Then it gave a shudder and picked up a double-time rhythm. The look of unconditional love he gave her caused hope to blossom. She looked away, not really wanting to know but unable to stop the word from passing her lips. "How?"

"Marybeth Ferris took great pleasure in telling me."

That zipped her eyes to his, shock making her jaw drop. "What!" she nearly screeched again. "How did she find…" Awareness flashed through her. "It was her."

"What?"

"She searched my room. Found the papers detailing my medical history."

Realization dawned. He said, "That's why no one thought anything. Everyone is so used to her being in that house, they don't even look at her anymore."

Feeling violated all over again, she shuddered. "I hate it when someone invades my space like that." She snapped her fingers. "The perfume. Dahlia had it on and

I knew I'd smelled it somewhere before. I bet Marybeth talked Dahlia into showing her which room I was staying in. Dahlia wears so much perfume, it lingered."

"Well, at least that's one question answered."

"One?"

"Yes, I still have another one for you."

She gulped. Why was he being so nice? He should be furious with her. She'd let him keep hoping there could be something between them while she'd known how important children were to him and yet she'd kept quiet. And yet, hope remained. He knew she couldn't have children and he'd still asked her to marry him. Still, guilt persisted and she felt the need to explain.

"I should have told you I can't have children when I realized our feelings for each other were moving beyond friendship. But you weren't a Christian at the time, so, to be honest it didn't seem like something I needed to bring up since I wouldn't let myself fall for you. And then we were thrown together in all this craziness that was my life…or I thought was my life, but was actually yours…and I was so focused on finding out who was after me…you…" She blinked, shook her head. "You know what I mean. I was so focused on that, that I just didn't stop to think about it. Avoided thinking about it. Put off saying anything to you."

He gave her a tender smile, one that took her breath away. What was the deal? He should be reacting…differently. She returned his smile with a wary look. "Why are you smiling?"

"Because you're you."

Anna blew out a half chuckle, half sob. "What does that mean?"

"You always think you've got to go it alone, don't you?"

"You mean until some psycho shoves his way into my life and forces me to partner up with him to catch a killer?"

"Yeah, but he's a psycho that's in love with you."

She turned serious. "Lucas, I can't have children." She'd said it out loud three times now. Maybe it would get easier. "If we get married, I'm so afraid one day you'll look at me and despise me." Her breath hitched on a sob, but she forced herself to continue, "And I just can't do that to you…or me."

"Look at me, Anna."

She did. Tears shimmered, obscuring her vision, but not enough so that she couldn't see the love shining in his eyes. He cupped her chin, pulled her to him to place on her lips the sweetest kiss she'd ever felt.

"I love you. For who you are, what you are and everything in between. I love your dedication to the children at the orphanage. I even love your fierce independence—although it does get on my nerves occasionally." He smiled at her hiccupped laugh, but turned serious and kept going. "I love the fact that you care enough about me to leave me. When I saw how determined you were to make sure I stayed safe, to the point of being willing to disappear from my life, I knew I'd never find anyone else like you. You understand sacrifice. You and Paulo. I saw Christ in you, Anna. I saw the unconditional love you offered Paulo, offered me. How can I offer you anything less? My love doesn't come with strings attached. It just is. Sure, it hurts that you can't have kids, but mostly because I know how much it hurts you. You are beautiful as is and I believe

God has amazing plans for us. Like adopting a little kid named Paulo who really needs a family."

Tears streamed down her cheeks as he spoke, ripping every last shred of uncertainty from her. Flinging her arms around his neck, she clung, weeping into his shoulder, the good one, and thanking God at the same time. Her crying jag finished, she pulled back with an embarrassed shrug. "Well, what do I say to that? Ditto?"

"That works for me." He helped her mop up, swiped a few tears of his own and their eyes met.

And they burst out laughing at exactly the same time. Anna leaned over to whisper against his lips, "We're a pair, aren't we?"

"Till death do us part."

The piercing shriek pulled them apart and around to see Paulo, well on his way to a hopefully normal life, vocally expressing his joy at the sight of the white playground. "Miss Anna, Dr. Lucas, merry Christmas! It's snowing!"

Lucas laughed at the child's unmitigated happiness.

Ever since clearing up the criminal investigations, he knew Anna had been investigating another possibility. Adopting Paulo. Lucas agreed without question that the child belonged with them. If he could ever get the woman to say yes to his question.

Eyes sparkling like rare jewels, Paulo took it all in, completely still in his dumbfounded awe. Dressed in a heavy winter down coat, hat, gloves and waterproof pants and boots, the child was as protected as he could be against the cold. Tentatively, he moved toward the fun, hands outstretched. He pulled off one glove and sank small fingers into the white powder, squealing, "It's cold! Let's build a snowman."

With Anna's help they soon had a round, white, three-tiered man with Lucas's cap on his head, two eyes made from brown leaves and a broken stick for a nose. Pebbles from the gravel walkway became a huge, dotted smile below the stick. The smile was almost as big as Paulo's.

As the snow started to fill in the patches they'd created while making the snowman, building the powdery stuff back up, Paulo grinned, giggled and sat down in the middle of it. He then stretched out on his back, swinging his arms to make wings for a little Paulo snow angel.

Lucas burst out laughing, ran and landed with a thump in the snow beside Paulo. A white mist flew up and splattered Paulo in the face. The boy couldn't stop laughing and Lucas felt his throat clog. *Thank you, God.*

He looked up at Anna, who'd waded into the stuff. Grabbing her hand, he yanked and, with a shriek, she landed beside him. "Hey! My pants aren't waterproof, you goof! It's cold and I'll be frozen."

"But you've thawed my heart, Anna," he whispered, turning serious, every sight and sound fading except for the vision of loveliness before him. "I love God and I love you. And you *still* haven't answered my second question. Will. You. Marry. Me?"

She gulped. "Are you sure? More than sure?"

"We've been over this. I won't say it doesn't matter because I know it does…very much…to you. But we'll work it out. We can adopt. I know of an orphanage full of children who need a mom and dad to love them…and teach them about the love of Christ, too. Starting with that little boy right there. Marry me," he insisted.

Tears dripped down her chin, salting the snow, melting it where they dropped. She nodded, blinked away the tears and grinned. "Yes, absolutely yes. I want that more than anything." Lucas pulled her down to him and planted a kiss on her starting-to-turn-blue lips.

She laughed against his mouth, her warm breath filling him with joy, longing and a thankfulness he never thought he'd ever feel.

Paulo's sweet giggles brought them around to see doctors, nurses and other hospital staff standing in a semicircle around them. Anna blushed furiously and Lucas cleared his throat. "Ah, well…um…yeah. Hey, she said, yes!"

Laughter and applause broke out, and Paulo looked up at Lucas. "See, God does answer prayers."

Dear Reader,

I hope those of you familiar with the Carolina coasts won't hold it against me for taking some license with the landscaping. Haven and Rocking Wave Beach are both fictitious towns straight from my imagination, and I certainly had fun creating them.

As this story developed, it occurred to me that a lot of what I was writing could have a double meaning. Hence the title *Holiday Illusion*. Lucas and Anna kept focusing on Anna's past and the people that could possibly want her dead, while all along it was Lucas who was in danger. Sometimes in life I find that I get so focused on one thing that I don't see what it is I really need to see until I stop and take the time to pray and seek God's guidance. I hope some of you can relate.

I'm often online at www.lynetteeason.com, and I love to hear reader responses. Let me know what you think. Until next time…

Lynette Eason

QUESTIONS FOR DISCUSSION

1. Lucas and Anna were doing good work in the jungles of Brazil. Do you think it was wrong for them to leave? Why or why not?

2. What do you think about Paulo and his unwavering faith in God and Anna? Do you know anyone with faith like that?

3. How does your faith in God compare to Paulo's and Anna's?

4. Why do you think Lucas and his father butted heads so much? Why do you think what was important to Lucas was so different from what was important to his father?

5. Growing up, Godfrey was jealous of Lucas and Lance. He's a prime example of what can happen when you allow something wrong to consume what and who you are. How can this adversely affect someone? What are ways to overcome jealousy?

6. Anna and Lucas had a lot of bad stuff happen to them. Yet Anna never blamed God. How did that influence Lucas?

7. Anna desperately wanted to fall in love with Lucas, but wouldn't allow herself that kind of relationship with him because he wasn't yet a believer. How do you feel about that? Do you think she made the right decision?

8. Who did you think the "bad guy" was? And were you surprised when it turned out to be Lucas's cousin? Why or why not?

9. What was your favorite scene in the book? Why?

10. Do you think Anna was right in keeping her barrenness from Lucas for so long? Did you like his response when he found out?

11. Do you feel Anna was too stubborn for her own good when it came to asking for help? Or do you feel she did the right thing and was trying to keep the people she loved safe?

12. What are your thoughts about Paulo's prayer right before he went into surgery? What kind of impact would that prayer have had on you if you were Lucas?

13. Sometimes we get something in our minds that takes all of our attention and pulls our focus from the main thing—God. What happens to us when we allow that? Do we end up getting blindsided, then wind up wondering what happened? What do you think God thinks about that?

14. Did you like how the book ended? Why or why not?

Love Inspired®

Eden, OK

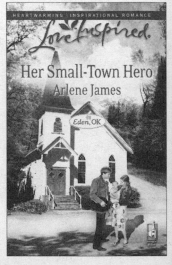

Oil rigger Holt Jefford is relieved when lovely Cara Jane Wynne applies for the job at his family's motel—so he can get back to his real job. But he soon senses the single mom is hiding out in Eden, Oklahoma. Cara Jane is scared of her own shadow…but luckily, Eden comes with its own personal small-town hero.

Look for

Her Small-Town Hero
by
Arlene James

Steeple
Hill®

LI87507

REQUEST YOUR FREE BOOKS!

2 FREE RIVETING INSPIRATIONAL NOVELS
PLUS 2 FREE MYSTERY GIFTS

Love Inspired®
SUSPENSE

YES! Please send me 2 FREE Love Inspired® Suspense novels and my 2 FREE mystery gifts (gifts are worth about $10). After receiving them, if I don't wish to receive any more books, I can return the shipping statement marked "cancel". If I don't cancel, I will receive 4 brand-new novels every month and be billed just $4.24 per book in the U.S. or $4.74 per book in Canada, plus 25¢ shipping and handling per book and applicable taxes, if any*. That's a savings of over 20% off the cover price! I understand that accepting the 2 free books and gifts places me under no obligation to buy anything. I can always return a shipment and cancel at any time. Even if I never buy another book, the two free books and gifts are mine to keep forever.

123 IDN ERXX   323 IDN ERXM

Name	(PLEASE PRINT)	
Address		Apt. #
City	State/Prov.	Zip/Postal Code

Signature (if under 18, a parent or guardian must sign)

Order online at www.LoveInspiredSuspense.com
Or mail to Steeple Hill Reader Service:

IN U.S.A.: P.O. Box 1867, Buffalo, NY 14240-1867
IN CANADA: P.O. Box 609, Fort Erie, Ontario L2A 5X3

Not valid to current subscribers of Love Inspired Suspense books.

**Want to try two free books from another series?
Call 1-800-873-8635 or visit www.morefreebooks.com**

* Terms and prices subject to change without notice. N.Y. residents add applicable sales tax. Canadian residents will be charged applicable provincial taxes and GST. Offer not valid in Quebec. This offer is limited to one order per household. All orders subject to approval. Credit or debit balances in a customer's account(s) may be offset by any other outstanding balance owed by or to the customer. Please allow 4 to 6 weeks for delivery. Offer available while quantities last.

Your Privacy: Steeple Hill Books is committed to protecting your privacy. Our Privacy Policy is available online at www.SteepleHill.com or upon request from the Reader Service. From time to time we make our lists of customers available to reputable third parties who may have a product or service of interest to you. If you would prefer we not share your name and address, please check here. ☐

LISUS08R

Love Inspired®
SUSPENSE

TITLES AVAILABLE NEXT MONTH

Don't miss these four stories in December

DOUBLE THREAT CHRISTMAS by Terri Reed
The McClains

She had means, motive, opportunity—of course
Megan McClain is accused of double homicide. But Megan
isn't willing to spend Christmas in jail for a crime she didn't
commit. And nothing Detective Paul Wallace says will stop
her from finding the killer herself—at any cost.

SEASON OF GLORY by Ron and Janet Benrey
Cozy Mystery

Why would anyone poison a holiday tea party?
Andrew Ballantine knows his would-be killer is still
in Glory, North Carolina. And to thwart the culprit,
he'll have to get well. Which means letting lovely nurse
Sharon Pickard closer than he'd like....

SUSPICION by Ginny Aiken
Carolina Justice

When Stephanie Scott is mugged, longtime admirer Sheriff
Hal Benson rushes to the pharmacist's aid. But then drugs
go missing, and Steph's reputation is at stake. Will Hal risk
his future to save hers?

DEADLY HOMECOMING by Barbara Phinney
All of Northwind Island believes Peta Donald murdered
her ex-boyfriend. No one thinks she's innocent except
newcomer Lawson Mills. And since no one's looking for
the real killer, only *they* can find the truth—before
the killer acts again.

LISCNM1108